Salsa SERENADE

Sylvia MENDOZA

Cover Design and Interior format by The Killion Group
http://thekilliongroupinc.com

DEDICATION

There is power in a group of women who don't even know their own strength. With compassion, perseverance, wisdom, drive, heart and vision, they inspire while getting the job done. I speak of my writing group. They've each faced incredible hardships and dealt with them, all the while holding onto their writing as an anchor. These women are solid and successful, nurturing and risk-taking, wise and accountable—and believe in follow through.

They've pushed me to leave my comfort zone and venture into new realms in publishing. So here I am again because of them. A special shout out goes to: Ara Burklund, Ann Collins, Judy Duarte, Chris Marie Green, Cheryl Howe, Mary Leo, Lorelle Marinello, Cathy Yardley, and Janet Wellington. Onward!

IN MEMORY

In memory of my Uncle Panchio, a handsome, proud family man with a true mischievous twinkle in his eyes and the ability to make me laugh on the darkest of days. He's what heroes are made of. I miss you, Uncle.

CHAPTER ONE

The salsa music wasn't loud enough, even though the floor vibrated beneath Julia Rios' high-heeled sandals. She closed her eyes and smiled, not minding one bit the way the backs of her thighs stuck to the uncomfortable folding chair. She inhaled deeply, taking in the beat until her body surrendered to it, and the muted chattering and laughter around her faded clean away.

This was bliss. If she could have, she would have cranked up the iPod speakers even louder and taken to the dance floor. Her aunt had taught her well. Salsa was not only a delightful dance, it was creative expression. Life. And escape.

As long as the rhythm ricocheted off the stucco walls of her aunt's dance studio, she was safe from any questions about her breakup with Francisco "Cisco" Valdez, one of the most eligible bachelors in town. He'd been quite the salsa dancer, she'd give him that.

Here she was safe. Certainly no one in their right mind would approach her at this decibel level.

She opened an eye a fraction to take a peek, and then quickly shut it. "Lord, help me," she murmured.

The room was quickly filling. When word had leaked that she had enrolled in her aunt's salsa class, enrollment doubled. Julia had dragged juicy scandal, a real live soap opera, right to their front doorstep.

The youngest in the room by twenty years, Julia was surrogate daughter to the students streaming into the quaint room. They were more like an extended family of aunts and uncles. In their eyes, she had to answer to them.

Julia didn't have much hope for keeping them at bay for long. Her smile disintegrated at the realization.

As soon as the music stopped, they would demand details of her sorry love life, an added perk for their money. They expected explanations and the right to confront her, swearing to help her find justice. All in the name of love, of course.

Elvira was ecstatic. Not for Julia's misery, but for the first time in years, a waiting list had formed. Julia was the best thing to happen to the studio since the Lopez twins had actually met the actor, Benjamin Bratt, at Lindbergh Airport three years before.

Glad that business had skyrocketed for the studio yet again, Julia resigned herself to being the ultimate advertising campaign for her aunt. Elvira needed the break financially.

For the twentieth time, someone patted Julia's head.

Julia reluctantly opened her eyes. "Oh. Hello, Lorenza," she mouthed at the elderly woman who lived across the street, her aunt's eternal student and best friend.

The only one to brave the music, Lorenza leaned close to Julia's ear and shouted, "Did he dump you?"

Why had Julia thought a little loud music would deter anyone like Lorenza? Julia expected everyone in the room to lean forward for her answer. When no one else reacted, she pulled Lorenza's wrinkled hand off her head and held it. She shook her head, unwilling to shout back a response because with her luck, the music would stop smack in the middle of her feeble attempt at explaining.

The sympathetic look in Lorenza's dark eyes—highlighted with fluorescent blue eye shadow today—said it all. She didn't believe Julia.

She took Julia's face between her hands and kissed her forehead. "Poor baby." Her whisper seemed as loud as her shouting. "That scumbag! If he wants to be mayor, he better clean up his act. None of us will vote for him if he hurts you."

She yelled again, "I want to hear every detail!"

Julia nodded. Her time had run out.

Lorenza bade her goodbye and paraded before the row of occupied chairs, her short party dress swishing around full legs. She greeted everyone along the way with smiles and touches and hearty embraces. She found a seat at the end of the row and stashed her white patent-leather handbag underneath it. Immediately, several older gentlemen surrounded her, nobly ignoring the loud music to attempt conversation.

Her reverie crumbled when she caught Elvira's dour look, aimed, she was sure, at her. Maybe Julia had cranked the music up a little louder than bearable. She glanced around and discarded that thought. She and Elvira were probably the only two in the room who didn't need hearing aids.

Julia blew her a kiss. Elvira wagged a finger at Julia and smiled.

Elvira's ever-elegant ballerina body glided across the scarred but gleaming wood floor to the IPod. She barely turned down the music. The buzz of countless conversations grew loud again. She opened a folder and leaned over the table, studying its contents.

At sixty, with her hair pulled back into a sleek chignon, she sometimes looked younger than Julia's mother. She certainly was more approachable and less likely to stay disappointed in Julia's fiascoes or shortcomings than her mother.

Not only had Julia broken off her engagement to Cisco—the charismatic front-runner for the upcoming mayoral race—she'd also left his father's prestigious public relations company. Many would call her a fool.

Julia glanced around. If there was one place where she could melt into the woodwork, it was here in the studio, her home away from home. Her aunt's students would let her get her shaky self standing again. Then they'd smack her on the butt and tell her to get back to the task of living.

She looked up and her spirits instantly lifted. She couldn't help but smile and wave at the gentleman approaching.

Her grandpa returned the wave and walked toward her, his steps long and sure. His smile reached his eyes, twinkling behind horn-rimmed glasses. His silver hair was slicked straight back from a high forehead.

Julia reached up and grabbed his hand. "Save me, Grandpa."

"Ah-ah-ah. You had to know it would be like this, *mija.*" He pulled around the chair she'd been saving for him so that he could face her.

She held his hand tightly and leaned forward until their foreheads almost touched. "I did the right thing, Grandpa, I know I did. Everyone thinks I'm a fool, giving up Francisco's name and fame, but it wasn't important. I want that all-consuming love. Passion, friendship, respect. Everything."

"Everyone thought you had that."

She sighed. "So did I. Francisco is a great guy, but there just wasn't that spark. Besides, I would never have been as important to him as his next campaign. I want to love somebody the way you loved Grandma, and have somebody love me back just as much."

His eyes misted. He slowly rocked back and forth, memory taking him far beyond Julia, even though it had been years since Grandma had passed away. "Ah, yes, *mija.* That once-in-a-lifetime love that makes you thank God daily and often times, count the hours until you're in each other's presence again." He closed his eyes and rocked again. "Yes, yes. But that's a gift, Julia. Just wanting it will not make it so."

Julia wanted to kick herself for changing the mood so drastically. "I guess I'm not ready, then. Setting up my company is taking most of my time these days."

He shook his head. *"Chiquita.* Timing has nothing to do with when you fall in love. It's not something to be negotiated or planned out."

"I know." Julia patted his hand. "I know, Grandpa. For now, I just want to forget everything for four hours a week, right in this room. Promise you'll be my dance partner."

He chuckled, the sparkle returning to his eyes. "Your aunt wouldn't allow that. Nor would I. You're going to have to face them all sooner or later. You'll feel better when you help your aunt. Dance with everyone here. Switching partners is what makes this fun." He leaned forward in his seat and waved at a tiny woman in a flowered dress at the end of their row.

"I can see I'll get a lot of sympathy from you, Grandpa."

"Not in this room, with this music. But come on over for coffee and your uncle's *pan dulce* afterward, and I'll let you cry on my shoulder as long as you need." He patted her cheeks. "If you feel you did the right thing, you did the right thing. Marrying the wrong man for the sake of a name would have taken years off your life. Now just dance."

He kissed her, rose, and walked toward the woman in the flowered dress.

That's why Julia had resumed her lessons in the first place. Music was medicine. Dancing was just what the doctor ordered.

Elvira looked up from her paperwork, glanced across the large room, and smiled. As she reached for the button to turn down the music, the bright sunlight streaming into the room through the open side door disappeared.

Eclipse, Julia thought, until her eyes lit on ridiculously wide shoulders silhouetted in the doorway. She followed the long line of a man's body—a man's large, hard body—with mild appreciation. There was no mistaking the masculinity exuded in that simple stance. Masculine, manly, macho. All with a capital M.

The old men around the room collectively sucked in their guts, reminding her of a bunch of roosters with ruffled feathers. The women sat up straighter and tried to cross their legs.

Slowly, silently, every head turned to watch the imposing figure step inside the room. Conversations dwindled to nothing.

Ignoring her proximity to the volume switch, Elvira cupped her hands around her mouth and apparently yelled something to the stranger.

Sauntering toward Elvira, he removed his white Stetson. From behind his back he whipped out the largest hand-held bouquet of red roses Julia had ever seen. Fascinated by the response to his presence, Julia rested her elbows on her knees and her chin on her folded hands to study the scene around her.

From the corner of her eye, Julia caught Lorenza waving frantically from her end of the row to get her attention. She jerked a thumb at the man, winked at Julia, then gave an A-OK signal.

Mortified, Julia pushed as far back into her seat as possible. Avoiding any eye contact with Lorenza would be crucial until the man left the premises.

He stopped in front of Elvira, bent slightly forward at the waist, and shook her slender hand. She accepted the flowers with a warm smile.

The man stood taller.

"Oh, brother," Julia muttered. She glanced at the dreamy-eyed women in their chairs and felt terrible for the men.

From this distance, she couldn't deny the guy was a looker. She didn't have to be a bettin' woman to say he was clearly not from any San Diego suburb she'd ever visited. She'd kill for a PR model that made people react like they had to him and wouldn't have minded placing him in an advertising campaign for anything. Beans. Bora Bora. BMWs.

His jeans hugged long, muscular legs at just the right spots. Light skittered off a silver belt buckle that had to weigh ten pounds, which partially explained his exaggerated strut. He reeked ruggedness, but his seemingly custom-made boots and white Stetson screamed exquisite taste. Maybe that helped tamp down the overbearing macho streak that emanated from him like a heat lamp on the verge of shorting out.

Elvira laughed at something the man said. Maybe not.

Julia sat up straight, the music no longer working its relaxing magic over her. So he had charm to go with that body. He put on his hat and pointed at the door. The look on Elvira's face fell. Her eyes narrowed. She rammed her fists onto her waist. For all his smooth and mesmerizing moves, the man had obviously crossed the line with her aunt.

Ah, thought Julia, *lesson number one for the visiting cowboy—Rios women aren't afraid to stand up to a man, especially on their own turf.* And this was definitely Elvira's turf.

Julia jumped up, her aunt's anger reeling her in. She looked only at Elvira, the worry in her eyes turning them a stormy gray. "Is there a problem, Auntie?"

"No problem, Julia. Mr. Montalvo is a new businessman in the neighborhood. He introduced himself, thought we had business to do together, and since we don't, he was just leaving." She threw the roses on the table next to the blaring iPod.

"And who, darlin', might you be?" The drawl floated down to her, deep and sexy and unsettling. It reminded her of warm blankets and blazing fireplaces and endless hours. And it had no right to be here at a time like this.

"I'm not your *darlin'.*" She enunciated the word with as much venom as she could muster.

She turned slowly and found herself nose-to-chest, checking out the silver tab buttons on his pressed white shirt. She followed the line of buttons to the hollow of his neck, taking in the broad shoulders yet again. His eyes, even though they gleamed as rich and dark as the coffee beans Julia bought, shone bright with amusement.

"You upset my aunt."

"I didn't mean to. Honest, darlin'."

Yes, he could surely sell anything with the way his eyes looked through her. Julia found herself wanting to believe him—but luckily, he spoke again.

"I offered your aunt a business proposition. A profitable one, I might add, and I tried to be neighborly about it. I'd like to buy her studio."

Buy her studio? "Trying to buy a business that isn't for sale isn't my definition of neighborly." Julia's hands turned cold and she clasped them to keep from throttling him. "I'm her niece. And her public relations and business manager." She wrapped an arm around Elvira's slight shoulders.

Her aunt looked at her doubtfully. "As of when, Julia?"

"As of right now." She stroked her aunt's arm. "Don't worry about a thing."

His raised eyebrows were maddening. "Ah, you're the one I'll be doing business with, then." He placed the hat back on his head. "I'm opening a sports bar and restaurant, complete with a dance floor to feature live entertainment, in the vacant lot next to this property."

He whipped out a silver case from his shirt pocket, slipped a card from within, and handed it to Julia. *Ricardo Montalvo.* "I'm open to any input you might have to make this a business deal that'll make all of us happy."

Julia crumpled the card in her hand. "The studio is not for sale, Mr. Montalvo. Hence, no need for negotiations."

"Let's be civil about this and settle it like the neighbors we're going to be," he said, his quiet tone suddenly deadly serious. His placid expression was betrayed only by the twitch in his jaw.

Anger rose in Julia at what he was subjecting her aunt to. "Neighbors don't roll into a neighborhood and threaten change if they want to be part of a community. Why would you want the studio if you're opening a restaurant with a dance floor? Certainly you're not worried about competition. We wouldn't be in the same league."

He stroked his chin with a ringless hand for what seemed an eternity. "Certainly not. I need the space."

"You have the prime section of the lot. You can't possibly..."

"I'm not talking about the restaurant. We need parking space."

Julia's mouth dropped open. Of all the insensitive things he could have said, this proved the most ruthless. She glanced at her aunt, who had shut her eyes and stood like a porcelain doll, motionless and fragile.

Julia hugged her until Elvira responded, clutching the back of the silk sheath Julia wore. "I'm sorry, Auntie. I'll take care of this. Start class before the natives get restless."

"I apologize, Miss Elvira. I was out of line."

She nodded curtly. Her shuddering breath echoed in Julia's ear. "Thank you, *mija.*" She leaned back from the embrace and patted down Julia's tuft of hair. "The show must go on, right? Señor Montalvo, if you'll excuse me?"

Elvira turned off the music with the flick of a switch and clapped her hands. "In a circle, everyone. Boy, girl, boy, girl. Let's have some fun today!" She pasted on a smile and headed for the center of the room.

Julia seized the diversion. She grabbed Ricardo's arm firmly and turned him toward the door. "Get out."

He dug his heels in. *"Boy? Girl?"* He glanced around. "Does your aunt need glasses?"

Julia crossed her arms, restraining herself from throwing him out physically. Her anger would give her strength to toss him right to the middle of his damned lot. "Don't go there."

"Darlin', it's a joke." He held up his hands in surrender. "All right. A bad joke. I'd like to stay awhile and watch, though."

"Impossible."

"I might want to take some classes."

"They're full."

"A waiting list?"

"Long."

"I want to learn salsa, officially. I'm a quick study."

"You don't look like the salsa type."

"What type do I look like?"

Julia let out an exasperated breath. "You don't want to know. Is this your idea of a business tactic—trying to force your way into the studio any way you can?"

"Nope. Your aunt called for fun. I need an intro to the neighborhood and a diversion from work. You know, all work and no play makes Jack a dull boy."

"You terrorize people for a living. I don't think that qualifies as dull."

"I'll pay private-lesson rates."

The mention of money fueled Julia's anger. "Go somewhere else. Your money's not wanted here. Please go."

He studied her for a long moment, the smile fading from his lips. "As you wish."

He walked past her toward Elvira in the middle of the dance floor, the swagger of his hips impossible to ignore. Julia's grandfather met him halfway to Elvira.

"I'm Carlos Rios. May I help you, son?"

"I just wanted to say my goodbyes."

"My daughter and granddaughter seem upset. Don't you think you've said enough already?"

"Apparently I have." He stuck his hand out and waited until Carlos took it firmly in his own. "Ricardo Montalvo. I apologize, sir, but I still have to speak to Miss Elvira. Excuse me."

He continued past Carlos, Julia close at his heels.

"Miss Elvira?" His voice boomed above her instruction and everyone stopped mid-step in their salsa lesson.

He took his hat off with a flourish and held it to his chest. "I apologize for interrupting your class and any grief I may have caused you. It certainly wasn't intended. I'll speak with your niece about the business proposition, but if you have any questions whatsoever, I'm at your service."

Elvira nodded. "Thank you."

He turned to the others. "Good day, folks. You're looking good out there. Maybe I could get a lesson sometime."

Lorenza stepped out of the crowd. She squeezed his biceps and patted his chest.

"I'd give you lessons, son, but Julia is a much better teacher."

"I don't think Julia likes me much," he whispered conspiratorially.

"She doesn't like any man much right now." She tugged his arm until he leaned down. "As a matter of fact..."

Julia stepped between them. "As a matter of fact, you're losing dance time, and Mr. Montalvo was just leaving."

She tugged his arm free from Lorenza's grasp and with a slight push, nudged him toward the open door.

He waved. Much to Julia's chagrin, everyone waved back in silence.

"You're not being very neighborly, Niece."

"And you are?"

"You can conduct business and still be a good neighbor."

"To you, this might be parking lot material, but to my aunt, this is her lifetime. Her heart and soul have made it what it is."

Outside, she wanted to smack the smirk right off his face. "Look around you. This is their only recourse for socializing in this neighborhood. It's within walking distance from their homes. I hate to think what would happen if you took this from them."

Slowly he crossed his arms and glanced around. "I admire what you're trying to do, really I do, but there's no room for emotion in a business transaction."

"Do you know how utterly ridiculous you sound? Every business transaction involves people. There's plenty of emotion involved."

"You want emotion? Take off your blinders. How much longer will your aunt be able to do this? Don't you want to see her retire with a comfortable nest egg? I'm offering to buy the place. I'll pay handsomely." He tilted back the Stetson. "This studio is quaint, but people are screaming for my kind of place, where they can really kick up their heels to do some salsa and two-step." He paced a few steps, then stared at her as if he didn't see her. "How about if I keep your aunt's building intact but move it from this lot? That's an option."

"No. It's a historical landmark, for crying out loud." Fear rose in Julia. This wasn't just another business deal she was making. Her aunt's life was at stake.

"Darlin', I'll be straight with you. There are more loopholes in your aunt's ninety-nine-year lease than you can imagine. My lawyer handed it back to me within half an hour, saying it was a joke. I could go that route, but I won't because I'm moving into the neighborhood and I'm basically a nice guy."

He pulled his hat down lower, shading his eyes. "On the business side of things, I've already covered my bases, dropped a ton of money into a can't-lose investment, and have political backing for the project. Let there be no doubt about it, Julia. I need my restaurant chain to continue to prosper, for reasons I will not divulge. Nothing's going to stand in the way of that. I will have that continued success right here in Old Town, with your help or without it."

He clamped his mouth shut, fuming, his chest rising and falling; Julia imagined it was his own control mechanism kicking in. Even though her knees knocked and she feared he would glance down and see them, she conjured up the most nonchalant look she could muster. She tilted up her chin. "Without. In Texas you might get everything you want by intimidating smaller businesses, but here—not so much."

His jaw twitched again. "Now, don't be hasty, darlin'," he said. "I didn't mean to spout off, but I want you to know where I'm coming from. It would be better for your *aunt* if you cooperated."

Her stomach was doing flip-flops a hundred times a minute. "The businesses in this neighborhood have been here for years. No outsider is going to tell them what to do or change anything just because you wave a wad of bills beneath their noses. We don't need a disco here."

"You need it more than you think. I've already talked to some local politicians, and they're eager to get this underway. It'll help your economy. It'll help give this area a contemporary look. It'll help bridge old with new. Don't make this difficult for your aunt. I'm requesting your presence in my office Monday morning. Give me fifteen minutes and I'll change your lives—for the better. I promise, and I'm a man of my word."

In less than fifteen minutes, he had already changed their lives. Giving him forty-eight hours? Julia shuddered, thinking of what he might do if she didn't show. For her aunt's sake, she had to go. "On one condition."

He shoved his hat back on and raised an eyebrow. "Negotiations already? My type of woman. Shoot." His disarming smile didn't warm her one bit.

"I want our meeting recorded and in writing."

"Easy enough." He turned to go.

"I'm not done yet." She straightened herself as tall as she could when he faced her. "Until we have a legal understanding of this business proposal, you stay the hell off of this property and don't come near my aunt again."

His eyes widened in surprise momentarily, but a slow, wicked grin tweaked his lips. He touched his finger to the tip of his hat. "Good day, darlin'. See you Monday."

CHAPTER TWO

The dozen or so keys on the oversized key ring jangled in Ricardo's hand as he neared his office. "A live one, that Julia." He chuckled. "Just what the doctor didn't order."

A woman like that made his blood pressure soar. Literally. Business was business. He didn't cut businesswomen any slack. They usually proved to be more ruthless than men in the long run. He rose to the challenge like a salivating dog eyeing a twenty-ounce Omaha T-bone from across a crowded room.

"Excuse me. Did you say something?" An elderly gentleman leaned on his broom, just outside the bakery next door.

"I have this bad habit of talking to myself to think business through." Ricardo walked the few steps to him with an outstretched hand. "Ricardo Montalvo."

He shook his hand warmly. "Marco Rios. It's all right, son. I do the same thing." He stood taller and pointed at the shop with the big picture window touting specials of the day. "My wife and I own this bakery."

He patted his barrel stomach. "Thirty-five years of marital bliss, baking and eating. What a life."

They laughed.

Ricardo shifted the keys to his left hand. "So that's what's been driving me crazy. It smells great."

"We have the best bakery in Old Town. Probably in all of San Diego. We've even been featured in the newspaper." He beamed. If he'd had suspenders on, he'd have slipped his thumbs under the straps and snapped them.

"You must have a steady stream of clients, if your name and reputation precede you." Ricardo glanced across the street. Would those clients venture to his restaurant? He couldn't wait twenty years to make his mark on the community.

He stepped back near the curb to get a better view of the blue and white awning and the shop sign. *Panaderia Rios.* "Rios? Are you any relation to Elvira?"

"She's my sister." They both looked across the street, a new strain of upbeat music filling the air. "She sometimes gets carried away with the volume, but it lifts our spirits on the street. We could have a block party and she wouldn't even know she was providing the music for it." He chuckled and lifted the black-framed glasses higher on his nose.

"Quite a lady, Miss Elvira. And Don Carlos?"

"He's my father. Good, fair man. Caring. Retired military. Navy, forty years."

Marco gestured toward the high-backed wooden bench sitting in front of his shop. "Let's sit for a minute."

Ricardo followed him, slid back into the seat, and nearly sighed. His body seemed to mold itself to the chair, offering comfort and a place to momentarily relax his aching shoulders.

Years of wear were apparent in the high sheen on the gnarly wood. A bench this old had to offer medicinal cures to seep through its grooves and into his war wounds. It looked like Marco was having a grand old time watching him get settled. "War wound?"

"No. Just football." Ricardo rubbed his shoulder and shifted until he was fully comfortable. "You?"

"A couple. Vietnam."

For a few seconds, he seemed to look into the distance. Ricardo had nothing to complain about. Football was a choice. Injuries, a risk. Enlisting was a choice but going to war was not. "I'm sorry."

"That was a long time ago."

"Time doesn't heal all wounds. My dad served." And that was one reason Ricardo was in San Diego. To ensure that his dad would be taken care of, medical and loan bills paid, and his ranch remain his. "So, Julia's your niece?"

A whiff of some sweet flower wafted through the air toward them, overriding the delicious bakery scent. "Yes. Her parents own the gift shop on the other side of your office. We were hoping when the flower shop closed down that Julia would start up her public relations business right in there. Make this corner of the block our contribution to the neighborhood. Bad timing, I guess. You beat her to the punch."

Ricardo didn't know quite how to read the old man. Was he bitter about it or just stating a fact? "It's a great office. A flower shop? Now that explains the huge back room and why it smells like roses and twenty other flowers I'll never know the names for. Other offices I've moved into are musty and smell like my old locker room. How'd I luck into this building?"

"Juanita died. No children to carry on. Sad thing, really, but it's good to see some young blood in the neighborhood."

"Thanks." Ricardo cleared his throat. "She didn't die in the office, did she?" Some superstitions he couldn't tamp down, no matter how far he moved from his mother and sisters.

"No, no, no. But Juanita was determined to leave a sign of her existence behind. I wouldn't try to get rid of this smell. I think she ground flowers into the floorboards and woodwork to haunt whoever took over the office. Like a reminder to deal with others sweetly."

Marco smiled, sending a chill down Ricardo's back. Did he know Julia was setting foot into his office come Monday? "Business transactions are rarely sweet but they can benefit the people involved." He had tried to be a gentleman and was more than fair in compensation. *Would the Rios women ever believe that? Would Marcos or Don Carlos?*

"What kind of service are you providing the neighborhood?"

Service? Ricardo took off the Stetson, like tossing aside his armor so Marcos could see he hid nothing. He stroked his chin, the five o'clock shadow prickly against his fingers. "I'm building a restaurant across the street, in the empty lot next to the dance studio."

Marco squared his shoulders to face him directly. "We have many restaurants in Old Town. How will yours be different?"

A clipped tone had eased itself into place and Marco's eyes were sharp and shrewd with the question. Ricardo couldn't forget that having a bakery withstand over twenty years of competition meant the owner was a competent businessman, even if he looked like an unsuspecting, clueless grandfather on the outside.

"It'll be a sports-themed restaurant, but with a dance floor adjacent to the main building." He left it vague, wanting to gauge his response to the older man's reaction.

"Sports restaurant? In Old Town? You'll upset the order of the Mexican history here. Besides, there's one just across the valley. It's pretty successful and has been here a few years. Local football hero owns it and draws a crowd. You're not from around here, are you?"

Marco shook his head. Ricardo found himself shaking his own in unwanted unison.

"No, I'm not," Ricardo replied, rubbing the tight knot in the back of his neck.

"But that restaurant doesn't have a dance floor like what I have in mind. You all are dancers and could appreciate it." He hoped they all were dancers like Julia, Elvira and Don Carlos. "I could change the restaurant theme. It's not written in stone that it has to be a sports bar. I'll look around and do my homework." *What the hell would he create if it wasn't sports-based?*

"Hmph." Marco pushed himself back against the seat, absentmindedly tapping the broom on the clean sidewalk. "I hope you're not only gearing it only toward young people. I like a night out with my wife. Something we can walk to. Coming to dance every week would be great. Lord knows we've had our share of lessons from Elvira and Julia."

Dancing for seniors? Ricardo wondered how in the hell he could manage that and try and keep an upbeat, contemporary look to the place at the same time. "I'll see what I can do. Speaking of which, I have to get back to work now. Office furniture should be arriving shortly."

He wasn't about to mention his upcoming meeting with Julia. He stood and looked down the street and back at Marco's unwavering, patient stare. He had a feeling Marco would know the entire gist of his encounter with the Rios women by the end of the day.

"Marco, it was indeed a pleasure talking with you. Don't be surprised to see me in your shop almost daily." *If you don't throw me out after Monday.*

"I look forward to it, son. You look like a strapping boy with a hefty appetite."

"You're right, and my weakness for sweets hasn't helped keep the weight off since I left football."

"You played professionally?" The wrinkles on Marco's face smoothed out in delighted surprise.

Nothing like humble pie. So much for banking on his name and image to promote the restaurant. Maybe a different P.R. strategy would have to be considered after all. "A few years. My time was up." He rotated his shoulder and the popping sound irritated him. "Matter of fact..."

A couple strolled past them and entered the bakery. Marco whipped his head back and forth between them and Ricardo. "Can I get a raincheck on your story? I love football."

"Sure, Marco. Anytime."

"Take care, son. Come and visit sometime."

He entered his shop and his voice boomed out, "Good afternoon! A beautiful day for a stroll. Might I suggest some delicious *conchas* to make the day even better? Muted laughter filtered through the screen door.

Ricardo turned back toward his own office, unable to wipe the smile from his face. He jangled the keys in his hand, trying to put together a clearer picture of the Rios clan.

How could the hellion they called Julia be a part of this warm, old-fashioned family? She wouldn't be easy to charm if she was defensive about men, as the old woman had pointed out.

And talk about protective. She was too overprotective for her own, or her aunt's, good. A perfectly good deal lay on the table, and she didn't see it staring her in the face.

That face, though. Man, oh, man. He could use her in advertising and promoting the restaurants. Build the restaurants, show that face, and they'd come. *Good concept,* he thought and smiled.

The lock turned and he entered the makeshift office, a home away from home. Strains of the salsa music drifted from the studio into his desolate office, even at that distance. He closed his eyes. His feet moved easily to the rhythm. He'd been the black sheep back in San Antonio—

challenging himself to more than football
footwork and country two-step or swing.
Salsa came easily. Why he'd given it up
remained a mystery. Maybe it was time
to pick it up again.

Placing his right hand on his belly, he
held up his left and started the hip sway.
He could still hear his instructor's count:
one, two, three. Five, six, seven. Cross
body leads. The hammerlock. The steps
came back to him on the whiff of a
memory.

"You've been spending way too much
time alone, Ricardo," he mumbled. He
missed it. But to dance, he needed a
partner. *Julia*. Yeah, right. She would be
glad to teach him a thing or two, all right.

He stopped dancing and reluctantly
shut the door. Music was mandatory.
Medicine. Magic. It had brought him back
to life after his football career ended.
Dancing was therapy—more for his
psyche than his physical therapy.

Here, he'd splurged on a top-of-the-line
Bose with speakers that cranked, making
it the major investment for his office.
Music would help fill the long nights that
loomed ahead.

He crossed the room, tossing his hat
onto a wooden crate in the corner. The
system stood precariously perched on the
rickety table against the back wall. It

would have to stay there until his rental furniture arrived.

He sure as hell wasn't about to conduct business in this office without a little crooning from classics like Shania Twain or Gloria Estefan to ease him into it. He flipped on the power switch and equalizer and turned up the volume. Gloria's smooth voice sang of destiny and lovers finding their way back to each other.

Destiny? Thought Ricardo. The tune was great but the words made icy fingers rake against his neck. He tried to rub away that cold. Believing in destiny like that was a crock.

Julia came to mind, but he quickly shook his head. He wouldn't allow the thought of her or their meeting to interrupt his light agenda for the rest of the day. There was plenty of time to prepare for Monday.

All he wanted was the physical labor of setting up his office as he envisioned it. And to forget about business for a while.

Running his hands over his face and through his hair, Ricardo realized three things. That he was working too hard, because haircuts and shaving had gone by the wayside. That it didn't matter, because he had loved the luxury of longer hair and a sometimes-itchy beard. And that good music was medicine for the soul.

Someone pounded on the door. Ricardo glanced at his watch then turned down the music. That would either be Chase or the furniture delivery. Good. Brooding one more minute would drive him nuts. He needed a night out in a bad way, and knowing Chase, he probably knew all the hot spots in San Diego, since returning early from the game. He'd be ready at the drop of a hat. Ricardo swung open the heavy wood door.

Chase stood grinning like a seven-year-old who'd just left a frog on a teacher's chair. "Well, dude, it's about time you finally made it to the West Coast."

"Timing's everything." He heartily hugged Chase. "Dude."

"That Texas drawl with beach lingo?" Chase stepped back and leaned his elbow on the doorjamb. "We'll work on it. It'll drive the women wild. Speaking of wild women, I thought you were coming for a little rest and relaxation, before you got down to work."

"R and R? Me?"

Chase sighed deeply and shook his head. The long, sun-bleached hair was a fitting testament to his new lifestyle in Pacific Beach, a community not far from where they stood. He still had an impressive build, looking as tough as he must have appeared as an offensive tackle. Thank his lucky stars they'd been on the same team and Chase was damn good at his job.

"All right, all right. R and R. Let's call it revenues and returns, for the sake of not scaring you off. But you're not sitting on your ass in your room this time. San Diego's got a night life now. And the women are hotter than Hollywood wannabes. Let the good times roll."

Ricardo didn't want to give in to Chase too quickly; otherwise, he'd be at the office doorstep every night, ready to party. That life had grown old quickly once he started his business. He wanted more, but wasn't about to confess that to Chase. "I've got a lot of work to do. You do, too, if you're going to run my restaurants when I head back home at the end of the year."

"All work and no play makes Ricardo a dull boy," Chase muttered and leaned against the door frame.

Ricardo winced at the too-recent memory of using the same phrase with Julia. It had backfired. His tactics rarely backfired. "Jack doesn't know what he's talking about."

"Ah, man, let loose, Rick." Another blast of salsa music blared from across the street. Chase automatically started major shoulder motion. "Doesn't look like we'll have to go far for a good time." He started moving his body in what he thought were dance moves.

Ricardo scowled. "It's just a dance studio. I've been banned from the premises. Come in and shut the door."

"What? Who gets banned from dance studios?" Chase's blue eyes opened wide. He stopped shaking his body to the beat long enough to shut the door and follow Ricardo into the room. "Obviously you do. You get to leave San Diego eventually. Don't leave any messes for me to clean up." He sprawled heavily into the solitary chair in the room. "I don't even have an office yet."

"This will be your office—and it's nothing we can't handle," Ricardo said, gesturing toward the studio.

"I don't like the tone of that."

"Elvira Rios and her niece Julia give lessons in that little studio across the street. I offered to buy the place so I could have more parking space. They don't want to sell."

Chase pushed himself out of the chair. He stomped over to the front picture window and lifted the sheet that hung as temporary blinds. "Please tell me you didn't propose they sell with that smooth line about the parking lot."

Ricardo didn't answer him. Chase had long been his reality-check man. Except he hadn't been there to save him from making a mess of things and putting his foot in his mouth with Julia and her aunt. Looking into Julia's eyes had made him flustered. He was going soft, losing his touch.

"Geez, Rick. You don't go into a new neighborhood—an old neighborhood—and bulldoze it to replace it with bigger and better stuff."

He released the sheet and turned to face Ricardo. The features on his face hardened into chiseled planes, his eyes narrowed. "You forget where you are. This isn't some ultra-sleek Manhattan strip where wheeling and dealing are part of the game. You're talking about people who've probably been here all their lives. You're talking about women who hold this community together. Why do you wanna go and do something stupid?"

"It's business, Chase." He stood toe-to-toe with him, like old bulls pawing the ground. Any of his convincing arguments were lost on Chase, but he had to try to get his support before Julia showed up on Monday. "I promised to take care of the aunt, financially. She looks about my mom's age and could be ready to retire. Maybe this will give her the opportunity to do that sooner."

"And look what you get out of it. Prime property at a bargain, beautifying Old Town with a little more asphalt." Chase didn't bother to hide the sarcasm.

"Is that so bad? Look how it'll lift the economy here."

"A parking lot. Yeah, you're right. It'll be a real economic boon to Old Town."

"Grow up." Ricardo turned away before he shoved Chase or did some other insane thing he'd be sorry for later. "This is business. Look at it that way."

"It'll disrupt lives. Some places just don't need change."

"Most places do." He ground his teeth until he thought he could spit his fillings into his hand.

They stared each other down. Gloria belted out a conga in the background. The scent of roses filled the air. Not conducive to hardass business negotiations. How would he get rid of that scent?

"I'll run your restaurants," Chase said quietly, "but I won't be any part of displacing families." He took a deep breath, his lips a tight line of anger. "What if Elvira Rios were your mother, Rick? Would you want someone doing this to her?" He shook his head, staring at the ground. "When did the dollar get to mean so much to you?"

That did it. Ricardo whirled and shoved a surprised Chase back onto his heels. "You want to know when? When my dad lost his job, his retirement pay, and ultimately the frigging house!" Rick turned away from Chase and clenched the edge of the table. "Sorry."

He reached a shaky hand over to turn down the volume, only to hear the haunting destiny song. If ever he felt trapped, this was it. "Man, Chase. I'm going to take care of my folks the best way I know how. I want them to have everything they ever dreamed of, everything they ever saved for. That's all. I can give it to them and to my sisters, to the man on the street corner, just because I want to. It makes me happy, even though I know there are trade-offs. Always trade-offs. I can't help that."

"Rick, I didn't know."

"It's not important to know. Not one bit of that information will ever leave this room. Do you understand?"

Chase shoved his hands into his pants pockets and nodded. "Got it."

"Let's get back to the business at hand. Your points are well-taken, you know that, right? I listen, even when you think I don't. So I'll take them into consideration as the negotiations get underway. I will take care of Julia and her family. They all own some business on this street. They won't take too kindly to me once they know my intentions."

Ricardo rolled his shoulders, but the nagging feeling that his decision could have been wrong wouldn't roll off his back that easily. His gut was telling him to walk away from it, ride off into the sunset like a good guy like Chase imagined. But his reasoning brought him back to his own family. That was the only thing that made him need to push forward. "I want you to know the players in this scenario."

"You mentioned a niece—as in lollipop-wielding?"

"Nope. As in raving lunatic dancer with a mission, disguised in long legs and eyes that make you feel like you're drowning if you look too long. She moves to these salsa beats with..." He stopped, realizing he'd said more than he'd admitted to himself.

"Pretty elaborate description, considering you only noticed the potential of the business."

Ricardo glanced out the window. "She's hard to miss. She'll make her presence known here Monday, trust me. We'd better get to work."

"You used to be able to handle businesswomen with such charm."

"I learned my lesson. Remember Rebecca? Astute, sophisticated, and deadly charming. It didn't hurt that she looked like J-Lo."

Chase whipped a battered baseball cap from his back pocket and placed it soulfully over his heart. "Your downfall."

"Nearly was. Until I came to my senses."

"Just in the nick of time." Chase shoved the cap back into his pocket.

"Women are worse than snakes. Strike, clamp, kill."

"Oh, no. Not by a long shot. You weren't some poor, unsuspecting victim. The signs were everywhere with Rebecca. You chose not to see them."

"The one mistake I've made in my sorry love life and you won't let me forget it."

"Damn straight."

"Chalk it up to experience, then. It won't happen again." Ricardo walked over to the window and stood next to Chase. From this angle, the dance studio complemented the other businesses on the street, circa 1950s architecture. The details pointed to design by renowned architect Irving Gill.

Picturesque with its slightly aged white stucco and red clay roof tiles handmade in Mexico, the studio stood out more than the other shops. Ricardo felt it more than he could see it. He couldn't make out the patterns on the glossy white tiles that followed the clean lines of the front window, but bursts of vibrant color were apparent on each.

From the blue and white awning hung a simple sign announcing in elegant, understated calligraphy: *Elvira's Dance Studio*. A bronze plaque by the entrance heralded it as a historical landmark. A screen door made of intricate black wrought iron allowed barely a glimpse inside. Much like sturdy castle walls, it could easily keep trespassers out.

"Cute little place," Chase said simply.

"Hmph." Ricardo didn't need to hear that. It was charming. Someone's lifeblood. Julia's face infiltrated his thoughts. For a second. He had to focus on his own mission.

Character, he decided, is what made the studio stand out among the other tiny shops, seeming to seep from the decades-old walls. It was an inherent quality he worked desperately hard to instill in his own restaurants. Most of the time he pulled it off; sometimes he didn't.

Chase, his annoying conscience, walked back to the Bose. "Hard to imagine it not there."

Ricardo tried to imagine the place leveled, replaced by endless feet of blacktop. He couldn't. Man. He was getting soft in his old age. Or at least around Chase.

Football had been so much easier. Catch a pass. Run. Score. Caught or not determined the next move. Although he knew he had a Midas touch for business, life was much more simple back then.

He continued to look out the window, grateful that Chase read him so well and gave him space when he needed it. He was mesmerized by the hand-painted sign that hung in the corner of Elvira's front window. A list of the types of dance lessons taught there included ballet and tap as well as salsa and merengue, waltzes and swing. Written with red marker and complete with curlicues and hearts for the dots over the "i", the elaborate cursive reminded him of his sister's writing when she was a teenager.

Blatantly missing were country two-step and line dancing. He could fix that. He squinted to see whether Julia had erased them, by chance, after he'd left. No evidence of that. Besides, the sign looked as old as the studio.

Julia didn't seem shrewd, though it could be part of her plan. She had a fire in her, a passion he himself had lost sight of a long time ago. If he touched her, could she breathe that passion back into his life, into his work?

Where had that come from? He raked his fingers through his hair. Who was he trying to kid? Julia wasn't fighting for the studio. She was fighting for her aunt. He was doing the same thing for his folks. A sinking sensation in his stomach told him what a jerk he'd been to Julia. Whatever she thought of him, she didn't know he believed what she did—family first, business last.

Still, he could persuade her to see what his offer could do for Miss Elvira. And he wanted to see her passion in action. Passion simmering that close to the surface had to spill over into other areas of her life. He'd like to be there when it did.

"Earth to Rick!" Chase's sharp tone blasted through the room. "Geez, I've been talking to you for five minutes, dude."

"Sorry. Thinking strategy."

"Strategy, huh? What's she like?" Chase tilted back his chair, looking like the proverbial cat that swallowed the canary.

"Who?"

"The niece—Julia, was it?"

Ricardo couldn't run from Chase. He'd drive him crazy, following him around like a pest of a little brother asking "why" a thousand times, until he drove him to the brink of confessing anything rather than hear the question again. Better to face Chase head-on.

Chase brought his fingertips together and began tapping them, waiting in obvious delight. "Well?"

"She threw me off her property. What's that tell you about her?"

"Nothing. Unless she's related to Harry the Hunk and knows some of his wrestling moves. Your reaction to her intrigues me. Please, continue." He waved his hand like a therapist urging him on. "What's she really like?"

"She means business."

"Ah. Is that what you were thinking with that goofy look on your face?"

Chase would rake him over the coals if he knew what he'd been thinking.

He grinned. "I can hardly wait for Monday morning."

Relieved at the mention of work, Ricardo let out a deep breath, which relieved the pressure on his chest. "Good. Back to business. My desk. Now."

"Smooth change of subject, Rick. Who else will be there, besides the niece?"

"Francisco Valdez, the mayoral candidate for this district."

"How'd you manage that?"

"I did my homework. I have political contacts in Texas who know San Diego. They put me in touch with him. He also owns his own PR firm."

"Good. So you've set the stage."

They walked through the second doorway, next to the rickety table. Chase whistled through his teeth. "Now this is an office—it's huge." His eyes darted to the front door and back to Ricardo. "You'd never guess this place was this big from the storefront."

"That's why I love it. It's my home away from home. Have to do it right. By the time I'm done decorating the place, it'll be fit for the governor. Or you."

"Cool. What's in the back room?"

"Bathroom. No room for a Jacuzzi, but it has all the other amenities."

"I'm sure it does. Throw a mattress on that desk and you'd have a bed."

The desk stood in the middle of the room, its mahogany luster dark and rich against the Saltillo tile floor. Ricardo walked over to it, leaving Chase in the doorway.

Running a hand over the edges and then over the smooth, polished surface of the desk, he took a deep breath. "This used to be my dad's. He gave it to me when I graduated. When I left the team, I refinished it myself. I've shipped it to wherever I determined my next temporary headquarters would be. A little good-luck charm."

"Little?" Chase eased his large body onto one of the chairs facing the desk. "Only in Texas." He sniffed and looked around. "You do flowers in the same dimensions? Smells like a damn flower shop in here."

Ricardo grinned. "Man, you're good. This used to be a flower shop. Legend has it, the former owner put a spell on the place with her flowers, hoping to teach whoever did business from here to keep it sweet."

He looked at the incredulity on Chase's face. "Seriously?"

"Or some shit like that," Ricardo added.

"You better hope it won't bite you in the ass. Old Town is the birthplace of San Diego. Superstitions run deep here. You don't want to be jinxed or have a spell put on you."

"That has nothing to do with business."

"True. She didn't know you were taking over. The smell will be gone by Monday afternoon."

Ricardo threw him a nasty look. "You're walking a thin line, surfer boy. Let's get to work before the furniture comes. I intend to work you to the bone. You'll earn your keep around here."

Chase laughed. "No doubt."

Ricardo and Chase had finished moving furniture into place when a knock sounded at the front door. Pizza. Pain shot into Ricardo's shoulder when he reached into the desk drawer for his wallet. "Damn." He straightened and rubbed the tender spot.

Not exactly painting the town red tonight, but he was beat. "Come on in. Door's open." He finally retrieved the wallet.

He was starving and was waiting for Chase to finish his phone calls from the privacy of his office. Fast pizza delivery ranked right up there with a Hail Mary touchdown pass. Almost.

The heavy door dragged open against the carpet, releasing a fresh scent of roses. "Ricardo?"

Julia's voice wafted over him on the subtle scent. He liked the way his name sounded coming from her lips. He turned wordlessly, wallet in one hand, several bills oozing out of the other.

Julia stood just outside the doorway, holding a wicker picnic basket. She looked at him and then at his hands. Her expression instantly darkened. "Do you sleep with your wallet under your pillow, too?"

Ricardo stuffed the bills back into his wallet. "I thought you were the pizza guy."

"Gee, thanks."

"Speaking of pizza, would you care to join us for some fine Italian cuisine?"

"Us?"

"My partner in crime. He'll be running the restaurants in San Diego when I return to Texas."

She took a half-step backward.

Ricardo cursed himself. "I'm sorry. This isn't a time for business. It's nice of you to come visit."

Doubt seemed to flicker in her eyes, then quickly disappeared. "It's not really a social visit, I'm afraid to say."

She licked her lips, the soft red tint staying put against all rational explanations. "My aunt made me bring this." She held out the basket by the vine-like rope handle.

He started to walk toward her but took one look at her face and he sat right down. She looked like she'd rather be thrown into a bullring wearing red rather than step inside his office. "That's mighty neighborly of her. Are you learning anything?"

Julia tilted her head and studied him before speaking. "I think my neighborly manners are on an even keel with yours, don't you?"

"Touché."

She blew a puff of breath upward and her bangs fluttered. "My aunt thinks if we don't offer the traditional basket to the new kid on the block, it'll bring bad luck. For the sake of tradition, then, and to avoid the superstitious bad luck from raining on our heads or on the studio, may I offer my aunt's homemade tortillas, hot off the griddle?"

She set the basket on the floor just inside the door and pushed it in as far as her arm would reach, but no more. Her toes were a good two inches from the doorframe.

"Don't you think you're taking this a little too far?"

"I have my own superstitions."

"And I'm one of them?"

"I won't set foot in your office until I absolutely have to—on Monday, not a second before, not before I'm prepared, not before the sun has risen on that dismal day."

Ricardo stood and planted his feet far apart. The girl talked too much. "Is this part of your business tactic?"

"What?"

"Driving me crazy with your repetitive drivel?"

"Drivel?" Her voice rose an octave. "I knew I shouldn't have stayed a second longer than I needed to." She sighed dramatically, her patience obviously running thin. "It's an old advertising trick. Repeat the message at least three times in different ways to get the point across efficiently. Especially if you're dealing with people who aren't capable of understanding the first time around."

"I'm perfectly aware of that technique." He walked across the room to her. The roses were lost in the more fragrant aroma coming from the door—a wonderful mix of Julia and the tortillas.

He picked up the basket and handed it to her. His finger brushed against hers. She flinched but held her ground. As for his own finger, he should just as well have stuck it in an electric socket. "I really shouldn't accept this, under the circumstances."

She cleared her throat and tucked her hair behind her ear, revealing delicate silver hoop earrings. The curve of her creamy neck screamed for someone to caress it, kiss it, taste it.

Where the hell had that come from? Business, business, business. Thinking in threes, and thinking of her neck to boot.

She handed the basket back. "Please. For my aunt."

"Very well. Thank her for me." His voice boomed louder than he intended. He took the basket from her outstretched hand. "A smile would help make these go down better, prevent indigestion, brighten the atmosphere around here."

Chase entered the room and looked from Julia to Ricardo and back again. "Julia, I presume?"

She nodded. "You must be the partner in crime."

"Please. Call me Chase."

"Good to meet you, Chase."

"Are you contagious or something?"

"No."

"Then why are you standing out there while we're in here?"

"Long story that I'm sure Montalvo will explain later." She riveted her attention on Ricardo. "About the smile. Sorry. You have to get that from my aunt. I'm just the messenger, the reluctant middleman, the niece, dragging her heels to get this to you."

"I get the picture, Jule."

"It's Julia. I'll leave you to your dinner. Good night, gentlemen."

Ricardo set the basket on the desk and hurried to the door. He yelled after her retreating shadow, "Julia!"

She stopped and slowly turned around to face him. The setting sun silhouetted against her. The rich auburn color of her hair against her creamy skin made words die on his tongue. She was stunning, giving the sun's warmth and vibrancy a run for its money.

"Yes?" There was no annoyance in the simple word, just fatigue.

He leaned against the door jamb, wanting to brand the image of her in his brainless head. "Thank you. Really."

She nodded, raised her hand in a silent wave and walked back toward the studio.

What the hell had gotten into him? He shut the door softly, stalling, waiting for divine inspiration before facing Chase. "Looks like she's coming around already."

The raised eyebrow spoke a thousand words. "Were you in the same room, Rick? Get that goofy look off your face." Chase lifted the dishtowel from the basket and the wonderful aroma filled the room. "Sorry I interrupted, but it was quite a show. She's a looker and she's not afraid of you. Gives her points in my book. We'd better talk more strategy before Monday."

"Strategy's set," Ricardo growled, more angry at himself than at Chase. "Just be here on time."

The tortillas' rich aroma had filled Ricardo's own home growing up. He doubted the basket's contents could compare to his mother's. He sniffed them again, dipped his little finger into the side of butter, and licked it off.

"Could be a trick," he said aloud, though he hadn't meant to. "Poison, if Julia had her druthers."

Chase laughed heartily. "It would take a lot more than that to keep you down, buddy."

"Damn straight."

Chase grabbed a hot tortilla and juggled it between his hands. "Even so, you first."

Ricardo picked up the plastic knife and smeared a tortilla with the sweet butter. It melted on contact. Then he sprinkled the *queso fresco* on top. His favorite cheese topping. Miss Elvira had thought of everything for the welcome gift. Taking one more whiff of the incredible aroma urged him on.

He bit into half the tortilla and closed his eyes. Heaven. He was home. "If this is poison, what a way to go."

CHAPTER THREE

Reaching out a lazy arm, Julia pulled back the bedroom drapes a fraction to peer out at the picture-perfect dawn. Splashes of pink and orange crowned the softer shades of blue in the cloudless sky. "What a way to start a Monday," she murmured and rolled onto her back.

She slid under her thick comforter and wriggled into her warm spot for one more blessed moment. Her king-size bed was a luxury, her big-time extravagant indulgence. Not a morning went by that she didn't thank the heavens for it.

It even made Mondays more bearable. Julia groaned. "Except today." Wasting a perfectly good Monday morning with Montalvo was not the best way to start the week.

She jumped out of bed, suddenly anxious to get moving. She pulled on her workout clothes. The antique clock on the bedside table told her to hurry and made her regret the extra couple of minutes she'd taken to pamper herself.

She and her aunt had reviewed the business proposal and were ready with counterattacks for all possible offers Montalvo might come up with. As prepared as she felt to take him on, there were two glaring facts she would not veer from: Montalvo was bullheaded. They did not intend to sell under any circumstances. End of story.

She walked out the door of her small home that overlooked San Diego's Old Town. The breathtaking view still never ceased to amaze her and could change her mood for the better almost instantly. The Pacific Ocean to the west ushered in white-capped waves along deserted beaches this early in the morning. Rolling hills were the backdrop for the renovated, freshly painted historical sites—like the Victorian houses that lined the narrow street. The Presidio stood on top of another hill, easily visible with its stucco bell tower and red-tiled roof. A par-three, nine-hole golf course lay just south of the mission. Julia played the course once a week, bets and all, with Grandpa.

Running late, she could see him now— probably pacing outside his own home a couple blocks away, forming a groove alongside the little white picket fence.

She ought to convince him to pick another day for their shared morning walk. Mondays were impossible.

As she started on her way to meet him, she sighed. Impossible perhaps, but she wouldn't trade her treasured time with Grandpa for anything.

Montalvo's words about taking care of her aunt nagged Julia the rest of the way. When she had left her public relations job with the prestigious Valdez & Cohen firm, she had left her benefits behind, too. The nest egg Montalvo referred to was practically nonexistent, especially since she had used much of it to establish her own company. Several clients had come with her, but it would be a while before she stopped holding her breath every time she waited for approval on a client's new advertising campaign.

She looked up too late. Despite the hour, Lorenza and her neighbor stood guard at the corner, scrutinizing each early morning walker while chewing on the latest morsel of gossip.

Julia jumped behind the nearest cypress in someone's unfenced yard and held on to the rough bark as if it would make her invisible. She suddenly sympathized with movie stars who had to endure paparazzi. Lorenza was bad enough.

"Oh, Julia." Lorenza actually raised her voice, probably in hopes of waking the neighbors. "I can see your grandpa from here. He doesn't look too happy." Her ploys often worked and drew the audiences she wanted. She was the next best thing to a talk the latest morning talk show host.

Julia took a deep breath and stepped back onto the sidewalk before Lorenza could actually wake the neighborhood. "Good morning, Lorenza." Julia walked up the steep incline to the smiling woman and kissed her on the cheek, then greeted the other woman.

Lorenza held Julia's chin between her fingers. "You don't look too bad for the wear, even in the morning light." She patted her cheek. "Are you handling the breakup all right?"

"Yes, Lorenza. So is Cisco."

"It's a shame, really. It seemed you two were meant for each other."

"We were always good friends. We always will be. But that wasn't enough for a marriage."

"I would have made it enough. Mayor today, governor tomorrow. The White House in ten years. *Chiquita,* you may have made a big mistake."

"I don't think so." Julia peered over Lorenza's shoulder. Grandpa made a silly face and pointed to his watch.

She started walking backward toward Grandpa. "Gotta run. I'm late."

"What about the cowboy, then?" Lorenza shouted. "He looks delicious."

"Not my type."

"Never say never, honey."

Julia jogged off. The women's giggles bounced off her back. Wait until they heard Ricardo's story. Julia was in for one long summer.

"Hey, Grandpa!"

"It's about time, Julia. The day's half over." His tone held a serious note as he tapped his watch, but the laughter in his eyes made her wag a finger at him.

"Nice try." Julia glanced at her own watch, appalled at her five-minute tardiness. "Restaurants aren't even serving breakfast yet." She grabbed him in a bear hug and planted a loud kiss on his cheek. "I'm really sorry I'm late, but how about cutting me some slack? It's Monday and..."

"Shh." He stood toe to toe with her and studied her face. Placing his hand on her forehead, he said, "You don't look so well."

"I'm fine, Grandpa, just not looking forward to my meeting with that displaced cowboy later this morning." She linked her arm with his.

"He seemed like a gentleman to me."

They headed east on the street, the slight incline already getting Julia's blood pumping. "That's because he didn't open his mouth near you."

He shrugged. "It seems that you've already made quite an impression on him."

"How'd I do that?"

"He couldn't take his eyes off you. You'll have to be careful with that one."

A chill ran across her arms, and goosebumps formed instantly. His presence had been all macho wrapped up in confidence and charisma, topped with a wonderful scent and a look that made her feel like eating melting chocolate. She shook her head. And he wanted to buy her aunt's studio. "I can handle him, Grandpa. One way or another, I'm going to convince him he doesn't need the studio."

"Take his personality into consideration before you head over there today. I don't think Montalvo would have let you break an engagement even after a calm, civilized discussion like Cisco did. He'd be banging down the door to convince you to stay. And he'd probably succeed, charming you until you changed your mind."

She shuddered. "What an awful thought."

"I just want you to be prepared. The biggest difference between the two is Cisco knows his limitations with our family. Montalvo doesn't. Hell, I changed Cisco's diapers. He ate at our table more than at his own. If he ever hurt you, he'd still know my wrath."

She patted his arm. "He wouldn't hurt me. I think the timing on all this is good. His political campaign is flourishing and he can devote all his time to that now. He's the frontrunner."

"What?" Grandpa looked at her as if she spoke an alien tongue. "What has all that got to do with how you felt about each other? You would have been an asset to his campaign, but for his life, too."

She shrugged. "Cisco and I have been friends and business partners too long and know each other too well. We had to face the fact that a solid friendship didn't translate to everlasting, romantic love."

"*Ay, mija.* Really?" Grandpa couldn't seem to stop shaking his head at her. Patting her hand, he said, "Why did you consider marriage in the first place? If you have to rationalize too much, it can't be love. Your generation never ceases to amaze me. Please tell me you weren't going to sign a prenuptial agreement."

Julia figured it better to remain silent rather than admit the papers had been drawn up and notarized a year into the engagement. But one look at her grandpa's grim face, and without a word, he knew. Waves of embarrassment, shame, and longing roared through her. What was she missing? How could she have been so off the mark, thinking of love with so many stipulations?

Grandpa stopped walking and turned to face her. "Don't ever settle, Julia. Life's too short for that." He patted her cheek. "You did the right thing, not marrying this one, even though he's a good man. When it's right, you'll feel the most incredible joy and the most driven despair and the most chaos in your head, sometimes all at the same time."

He started to smile, but then his brows knitted together, pain evident in the creases between his eyes. Color drained from his face, turning it ashen.

"You'll..." His mouth moved, but the words didn't come out. He clutched at his chest.

"Grandpa?"

He squeezed Julia's hand unmercifully hard.

Julia threw her other arm around him to hold him up. "Grandpa!"

He pulled out of her grasp and waved her away. "I'm fine!" he gasped.

Julia flinched at his tone and hardened her own. "No. You're not." She reached for him again.

He slapped her hand away. "Yes. I am." He gulped a couple of breaths before he could slow down the movement of his chest.

Julia stepped back to give him space. Shocked at his reaction to her attempt to help, she rubbed the sting from her hand for lack of something to do. He had never reacted that way to her and it scared her. She blinked hard and fast until she was certain she could keep her tears at bay.

He patted the middle of his chest with the palm of his hand for a few more seconds. "It's that damn indigestion, that's all." Color had returned to his cheeks. His posture was stiff, as if he were struggling to keep himself upright.

Julia waited until he turned to her and looked into her eyes. "When's your next doctor appointment?"

"This afternoon."

"I'll take you."

He shook his head. "Only if you get your aunt's situation with Montalvo under control first. I need to make sure she's taken care of."

"And I need to make sure you're taken care of." She tried to keep the quaver she wasn't used to from reaching her voice. "I'm calling the doctor first. If she says you can wait, I'll finish with Ricardo and be at your doorstep before you know it. If you can't wait, Ricardo will have to."

"I don't want you worrying about me right now. We need to worry about your aunt. We need to worry about Montalvo. You need to devise an alternative he'll be happy with. I know you can do it. I can wait until this afternoon, and then you can worry about me all you want."

"It'll take me awhile, but I'll come up with a solution. I promise. We'll save the studio."

"Good girl. So, do you have time to cook me some breakfast?" he asked hopefully.

She linked her arm with his, painfully aware of how fragile his bones felt. "Of course I do. How about oatmeal?" Her voice was steady, casual even, though her heart was tight with fear.

"Anything but oatmeal."

"Why's that?"

"Only old people eat that mush on a daily basis."

"It's settled, then. We'll each have a bowl." Julia slowed their pace and turned up the block.

She held her grandpa close. If Ricardo didn't already know it, he would soon—her family came first. That knowledge was all the ammunition she needed and she wasn't afraid of facing him anymore.

Sunlight streamed into Julia's home office, hot and bright. Any remnants of the cool morning air dissipated with her growing apprehension at meeting with Ricardo. The newly made file folder with her questions and counterattacks sat atop her sleek desktop.

She was as ready as she was ever going to be. She took extra care with her makeup and chose scarlet liner and lipstick. A flimsy armor to be sure, but a necessary one. She grabbed the files, threw them in her briefcase, and locked it shut. The one block to his office would be a last chance to gather her thoughts and courage.

Ricardo's office looked deserted. Tapping on the door brought no response, and Julia shifted her briefcase to her left hand. She adjusted her blazer and the short skirt of her red suit. Not only was it her power suit, it lifted her spirits and confidence in one fell swoop.

She rapped harder on the heavy wooden door, scraping her knuckles, and she cursed under her breath. "Tactics," she muttered. She'd wait ten minutes and then leave. She banged one last time. "Montalvo!"

The door swung open. Ricardo stood shirtless. Drops of water dripped from the ends of his long hair onto his chest, giving it a light sheen. "Julia."

He crossed his arms in a seeming attempt to cover his chest, but it only accentuated his muscles. Julia swallowed hard. *Unusual tactic,* she thought, *and totally unfair.*

"You're early." He seemed genuinely uncomfortable, color rising in his cheeks. "I thought you were Chase. Come on in. I'm running a few minutes late, but there's coffee and *pan dulce* on the table. Please help yourself."

He stepped back to give her a glimpse of the pink bakery box she recognized instantly from her uncle's bakery. The coffeepot sat on the narrow table against the far wall from where they stood. "Are you looking for an in by using my uncle now?"

"Ow." He put his fist against his washboard stomach and yanked outward, as if she had stabbed him with a nasty old lance and he had to pull it out or perish.

"Do you ever give people the benefit of the doubt? I love this stuff and simply offered to be his guinea pig for a new concoction he was trying out. He, in turn, gave me half a dozen pastries."

"There has to be a catch somewhere."

"You tell me. What he whipped up was one of the richest sweetest things I've ever tasted. I'd love to get it on my restaurant menu. On the other hand,"— he lifted and lowered each hand as if he were weighing apples—"I should never offer my tasting services to a baker. I'm a sucker for dessert."

Obviously sugar does a body good. He was being way too nice. Julia narrowed her eyes to get a better glimpse of him beyond that body.

He backed up toward a doorway on the other end of the room. "Can you give me a few minutes?"

"You said ten o'clock and I have other appointments," she managed, glancing at the spare office, the healthy fern in the corner, the coffeepot, the NFL clock— anything and everything but his chest. "I'll give you five."

He stopped in mid-track, a raised eyebrow and maddening smirk adding more character to his face than a thousand-watt smile. "That's generous of you."

His sarcasm grated on her nerves. "Very. I charge a hundred dollars an hour for consultations alone."

"Is that all? From what I hear, darlin', you're worth much more."

"I'm afraid my family is biased."

He threw his head back and laughed, surprising her. It seemed like the hearty, rich sound was no stranger to his life or lips. It reverberated through her, making it difficult to rein in the smile that tugged at her own lips. She couldn't remember the last time she made someone laugh like that. Come to think of it, it had been a while since she'd heard her own laughter fill a room.

"So there is a sense of humor inside that pretty little body." He roped the towel around his neck, the muscles in his forearms and chest terribly distracting with each subtle move. "Five minutes it is."

As soon as Ricardo walked through the door toward what she assumed was his office, Julia set down her briefcase near one of the unopened pink boxes. She wiped sweaty palms along the sides of her skirt. Heading for the coffee with a surer step than she felt, Julia repeated her calming mantra.

She lifted the lid of the box and the aroma of the freshly baked pastries drifted through the air. She nearly sighed. How much did Montalvo know about her? Did he know that with her discernible sweet tooth she could be blindfolded at midnight and still find a box of pastries that was purposely hidden on the opposite end of the house, on the second floor?

"Unfair tactics," she muttered. She poured herself a cup of coffee and glanced at the sterling silver ice bucket to the right of the pot. It was filled with a variety of flavored creamers.

She poured the amaretto-flavored creamer into her coffee, grabbed a *concha* from the pasty box, and made herself comfortable in the only chair in the office. She hoped Montalvo would take ten minutes.

The front door crept open. "Rick?"

Chase stuck his head in and when he spotted Julia, smiled warmly. "Ah. A face I'd much rather see. How are you this morning, Julia?" He let himself in and walked directly to the food.

"Apprehensive, wary, prepared." She popped the last of her pastry into her mouth and refrained from grabbing her compact to check for any stray crumbs. She licked her lips instead.

"Rightly so." He grabbed two pastries and filled a cup with steaming coffee, no creamer. "Come on. Let's wait for Rick in his office."

She followed him but stopped in the doorway. "Wow."

"Impressive, huh?"

Julia inhaled deeply, the rich and powerful fragrance of a dozen competing flowers somehow working together for an exotic blend of heaven. She half expected to see the old woman working in the corner of the room, preparing countless arrangements with deft, efficient hands. "It smells incredible."

"Rick didn't know what to do about that at first, but he's gotten used to it. And I think he's a little superstitious, though he'd never admit it." Chase pulled out a chair near the massive desk in the middle of the room and plopped his pastries onto its gleaming surface.

She walked around the mahogany desk, mesmerized by the workmanship. She ran her hand along the smooth edges. "Great taste," she murmured, recognizing the attention to detail in the intricate lines.

"Thank you, darlin'." Ricardo's drawl wafted across the room. Fully clothed now, he looked striking in a deep navy-blue suit. The soft light in the dark room glinted off his Gucci shoes. He looked just as comfortable in a suit as he had in his jeans and boots at the studio. The double-breasted jacket accentuated his chest, that mighty diversion.

Chase glanced at Julia, then at Ricardo and back again. "Hmm. Mr. Power Suit, meet Ms. Power Suit." He chuckled and bit into his pastry, sending crumbs flying onto his jeans and onto the floor near his Nike-clad feet.

"You'll have to forgive Chase, Julia. He's brain-dead but still attempts humorous interjections from time to time." Ricardo tapped his forehead with his index finger. "One too many tackles."

Ricardo laughed his wonderful laugh again and walked across the room to his desk. He rapped a stack of papers on his desktop, straightening them. "Time to get to work," he said, unrolling what looked like blueprints onto the uncluttered desk.

Julia opened her briefcase. "As I said the other day, we're not for sale."

"Why don't you cut to the chase, Julia?" The smile threatened to reappear on his full, tempting lips but disappeared when she didn't respond. "If you'll step around here, I'd like to give you an overview of my plans. The vision I have for myself and for each community I build in goes beyond structures. I don't pilfer and pillage just for the sake of the game. I'm not a pirate. I don't need to be. I do try to be green and leave my mark in a way that can help the community, not hurt it."

"Chase?" She wanted his take on it.

"It's true. As far as I can tell."

She studied Ricardo, appreciating his candor as much as the line of his jaw, which gave him a rugged, chiseled look. She tried to ignore the smell of that damn cologne. He didn't sound threatening at all. Was it Polo Black?

"All right." She grudgingly got out of her seat. "Show me."

"I do try and bring something positive to the communities we build in." Ricardo gestured at Chase. "Once the three restaurants are built in San Diego, Chase will take over as general manager and run them while I move up the coast to L.A., San Francisco, then on to Portland and Seattle."

Chase studied the plans. "The restaurants will be my responsibility. The other two have been set up with no problems, since they are being built in vacant areas. I promise to take good care of them, and the communities they'll serve. You have my word, Julia."

"What exactly does that mean in our case, Chase? That after you level my aunt's studio and put in a parking lot, you'll clean up the neighborhood?" She inched closer to Ricardo to get a better look at the plans spread out on the desk. "Look at this plan. How are you going to keep the quaint air of Old Town here with a monstrosity like that?"

Chase scratched his head and took a sip of his black coffee. "It'll be built like the surrounding buildings, of stucco and red-tile roof, old wood doors. We do intend on blending in and preserving as much of the ambiance as we can. That's how Rick's set up his other locations."

The unflappable Ricardo pulled out another rolled-up, oversized paper. "Let me give you a better idea." He spread it out over the blueprints, and Julia saw that it was a map of the area.

The artist had created a beautiful rendition of a Spanish-style building—a big, oversized building. It looked like a mama bear surrounded by many little bears of the same look and caliber.

It's not half bad, thought Julia. "I see in this rendition that my aunt's studio is still standing."

"That's before I worked out the dimensions for the surrounding area. Look, we can move your aunt's studio right up the street to this other lot."

"Is 'no' a hard word for you to understand, Montalvo? This is the family corner, except for your office. Hers is a historical landmark right where it's at.

You don't just move historical landmarks to more convenient places."

"Julia, it's up the street for crying out loud, not on the other side of town."

Why couldn't he see how important this was to her and her aunt? To her family? "What would your mother say about putting an old woman out on the street, Montalvo?"

He narrowed his eyes and the fury in them made her want to take a step back. "I am *not* the monster you think I am. I take responsibility for my actions. I gave you my word that I would take care of your aunt. Money is only part of it. If you'd work with me on this, you'd see this is in her best interest, as well." He rapped the desktop with clenched fists.

Julia had no doubt he could have squeezed the air right out of any old football he happened across if she had finished her thought. Score one for Ricardo on self-control.

Chase cleared his throat. "We have a visitor."

Francisco Valdez stood in the office doorway. A look of mild surprise appeared on his face as his gaze swept across the three of them and landed on Julia.

Julia straightened and faced Ricardo. "Montalvo, what's the meaning of this? What's Cisco doing here?"

Ricardo looked back and forth between Julia and Francisco. "Cisco?"

She crossed her arms. "We're old friends. Family friends. And former business partners."

"You worked at Valdez and Cohen? My people put me in touch with Mr. Valdez. He's giving me the political backing I need on this project. He's agreed to help me promote the restaurant as an asset to the community."

She whirled to face Francisco. "You *what?*"

"Julia." His voice was soft and understated, showing its own version of self-control, compared to Ricardo's simmering fury. It only added to the tension. He crossed the room to her.

She allowed him to take her hands in his and kiss each cheek as she returned the gesture. "What are you doing, Cisco?" she hissed.

"This is my district. Mr. Montalvo sent a proposal to me months ago about the project." Francisco proceeded to shake the hands of Ricardo and Chase. He turned back to Julia.

A brief thought of conspiracy raced through Julia's panicked mind. "Months ago?" The realization made her stomach roll. They'd been together "months ago."

"Months ago, and you didn't tell me, didn't warn me then?"

"I didn't take him seriously until now, now that he's moved into town. He's going to build this restaurant whether we back him or not. I think it would be better for all of us if we support his project."

"This is my family you're talking about. It's amazing that your acceptance of the project happens to coincide with our breakup. Are you trying to get back at me? You need to leave my family out of this."

"Your breakup?" Montalvo stood taller and took a step toward them.

Julia threw him a look that stopped him in his tracks.

"It's not what it looks like, Julia." Francisco sat in the leather-upholstered armchair. "Please, have a seat. Let's discuss this rationally." His movements were as smooth as the creaseless pants of his Italian designer suit.

"I'll give you rational, Cisco. You've become the politician you swore you would never be."

Something flashed in his eyes, but his voice remained entirely calm. "That's not true, Julia, but I've had time to think about this, and I have to move on it."

Julia glanced at Ricardo, wanting answers to calm the chaos swirling inside her. For some insane reason, she knew he would be straight with her. "Why my family?"

Ricardo caught and held her gaze. "I didn't know Valdez had a personal stake in this, not that it matters. Personally, I would have told you months ago, whether I thought it was a viable project or not. I'm sorry you weren't informed earlier."

Heaven help her, she believed him. But she had also once believed in Francisco. The walls felt like they were fast closing in on her.

He glared at Ricardo. "Yes, well, I made a horrible mistake in not telling you, Julia. I truly apologize for that and will apologize to your aunt, as well." His soulful eyes pleaded with her, and he shifted uneasily in his seat. "Now that Montalvo has refined his business proposal, it's the best I've heard to rejuvenate this area. I think your aunt should sell him the studio."

CHAPTER FOUR

Julia stood between Ricardo and Francisco, fuming. "Sell the studio?" If Cisco wanted to get back at her for breaking the engagement, he picked a bad day to do it. "Why do you both think you know what's best for my aunt?"

Pitted as she was against the two powerful men, they might think they controlled her aunt's future, but they had no idea who they were dealing with. She wasn't about to give in. Not without a fight. Putting her life and passion into the studio, her aunt deserved the utmost respect and consideration. She had to decide what was best for herself and her studio—not be pushed into a corner to decide.

Julia rose with a deliberate, calculated slowness, giving herself an extra minute to think things through. She glanced at her watch, fully aware that she didn't have time to waste when her grandfather was home waiting for her. "Francisco, what's in this for you?" She leaned on the edge of the polished desktop.

Francisco cleared his throat. "I'm not selling out, if that's what you're thinking."

"You said it. I didn't. But now that you mention it—of course you're selling out, Cisco. My family practically raised you, yet you're willing to play a traitor. A Judas."

Francisco fiddled with the tight knot of his multicolored designer tie. "I love your family. I love... this area, but developing and updating it is on my platform. You knew that when you worked by my side. You believed in me. You promoted me. You knew my agenda. I measured the options. We can keep it as a historical landmark—just move it onto other Old Town premises. Don't underestimate me or how I value this community and your family. And you."

"You have a funny way of showing that." She couldn't stop shaking her head. "I don't know what Montalvo has offered you, but you've changed. I know you too well, and I can feel it."

Tired and frustrated at sounding like a broken record, she pushed a stray wisp of hair off her forehead. "The people here deserve more consideration. Most are elderly, many of them are friends—and all of them live and intend to die in this community."

Francisco looked like he was counting to ten. "This is my district, Julia. You think I don't know that?" He struggled to control his voice. "Your grandfather, your aunt, and you are part of my family. This is my community. I think what Montalvo has proposed will benefit all of us. Of course I thought of Tia Elvira when I decided to endorse his restaurant. With the money he's offering, she can travel, paint, and do the hundred and one other things she's always wanted to do with her life. You know that better than any of us. She's never had the opportunity."

Julia slapped her hand on the desktop. "Why do you two think you know what's best for my aunt? The studio's her life. If she had wanted anything else, she would have closed up shop years ago."

"Why do you think *you* know what's best for your aunt?" Francisco countered. "Have you even asked her? Does she even have the money to do what she wants? Or have you just taken charge without a clue as to what she really wants?"

Ricardo clapped in an exaggerated movement. "Bravo. Bravo."

He pushed back his chair and placed his feet on top of the desk. "Great opening statements on both sides. It gives me a clearer picture of how to adapt my proposal to fit your needs. Now, it's my turn."

His voice commanded attention. Years of business still hadn't prepared Julia for anyone like Ricardo. The heat and energy sizzling from his body merely reflected the way his mind figured, calculated, and focused. That one-track mind could help him pounce on any unsuspecting victims. She would not be one of them.

With a moment to gather her thoughts, she gratefully inched away from him and made her way back to the seat between Francisco and Chase. Instantly, she was sorry she did.

It put Ricardo in the spotlight and he shone brilliantly. He stood before them like a great lecturer, ready to expound on the latest theory of a newly discovered solar system. They sat, clumped together like awestruck students.

Ricardo pushed back his chair with a gentle shove from his muscular leg. "In a nutshell, Mr. Valdez agrees with my way of thinking. He's a visionary. Julia prefers things remain the same—to honor tradition and a sense of community. Safety in the recognizable, the comfortable. That isn't to say that's bad.

There must be a middle ground somewhere."

He seemed to have forgotten they were all in the room. His gaze fell on Julia and a spark returned to his eyes and voice. "Julia, I've gone about this the wrong way. I want to apologize right off the bat."

The scent of roses seemed to filter through the air vent. Caught off guard, Julia backed against her seat and opened her eyes wide. For Ricardo to use sweetness in his business dealings could simply be a set up for her to take the sting.

It didn't help that his drawl curled around her like a refreshing summer breeze, or that he looked at her in such a way that the other two men in the room disappeared like the last strains of a *bachata* or soft waltz. If he could dance like he threatened, no woman would be safe in his arms for long. *Lord, where had that come from?*

He paced the length of his desk. "I'll take a few minutes to explain my business plan, how each of you ties into the plan, and how I hope we can work together. There's room for your suggestions, of course. My goal is to come to a satisfying middle ground."

"Satisfying for whom?" The words slipped from her mouth before she could stop them.

"For me, primarily." He shrugged. "It's my business. We're talking financial gain and development of my restaurants. But I'd like for all of us to be happy in this proposal. Contrary to your initial opinion of me, I'm not always hardheaded or out to devour a community whole."

"Only ninety-nine percent of the time," Chase muttered.

Ricardo slipped his hands into pants pockets. The bottom of his jacket bunched up around his wrists. "You're not helping the cause, Chase."

He tried to scowl, but as soon as he looked Chase in the eye, the grooves between his drawn eyebrows disappeared. Almost hidden beneath the soft stubble, a smile touched the corners of his lips. "Chase has always been a great 'yes' man, as you can see. He'll look out for you two, even against my inclinations."

Chase snickered.

Julia glanced at her watch again. Time was ticking. She wasn't going to miss Grandpa's doctor appointment.

Ricardo looked at her questioningly and cleared his throat. "Julia, when I did my initial investigation of San Diego, this looked like the most promising area. I've never had a restaurant in an Old Town setting, or in a basic tourist area. This had the best of both worlds. Chase did some groundwork, the lot was available, and he gave me Francisco's name.

"Valdez saw the value of such an opening. It could draw a younger crowd, help the economy, even teach something of our heritage to those who visited.

"The only drawback was a lack of parking space. That's when I spotted your aunt's studio. When I checked into her background, I must admit, all I saw was her age, and that maybe, just maybe, she might be ready to retire. I was ready to offer a comfortable alternative."

Julia fought to stay rational, taking it all in. He'd left no stone unturned. She studied his face, the beauty of his dark skin and thick hair, and wondered how much compassion lay beneath the defined features of that maddening face and hardass body. If the sparkle in his eyes and the simmering sense of humor were any indication, there was hope.

"There's more than meets the eye, Montalvo. You saw her age and a building, when in reality she is an icon and her studio is a haven for locals." She rose from her seat and walked around the desk to stand before Ricardo, carrying her portfolio. The desk pressed hard against the back of her thighs. "Please," she whispered, "have a seat." She pointed, indicating the chair behind him.

Ricardo nodded curtly and did as she asked. Unbuttoning his jacket, he slid into his oversized chair, thick with soft leather cushioning and rosewood armrests. Tilting it back, he waited.

Given space from his overpowering presence, Julia's head cleared. "I'd like three months."

His chair dropped to its front legs. "Three months? For what?"

"That's how much time I need to come up with either an alternative for you or a retirement plan for my aunt."

She glanced at Cisco. "Or to fight all of you to the death."

Ricardo laughed without genuine mirth. "The dramatic suits you." The smirk returned to its maddening tilt. "If I give you three months, what's in it for me?"

Finally the idea jelled. "I'll give you ten hours a week of my time to develop your advertising campaign."

"I don't think so." He tilted the chair back again, stroked his chin, and finally shook his head. "I need quality work. Savvy, contemporary, fast-paced. You, darlin', seem to be stuck in Old World ways of thinking. And ten hours a week hardly suffices for a startup."

Appealing to his finer sense of judgment floundered. "I'm not stuck. Family values are important. My family's always been there for me. Now it's my turn to come through for them. I can make things happen with ten hours a week advertising or business matters. Advertising is advertising and I'm damn good at any campaign I undertake. You have my word I'd give you quality work."

She opened her portfolio on top of the blueprints and drawings. "These are examples of some of the campaigns I've produced."

"You're giving your word? That didn't work when I said it. Why should it work now?" He stretched out his leg and it brushed against her ankle as he leaned forward in his seat.

She stopped herself from flinching at the touch. "Stop playing devil's advocate. I'm asking for three months, during which time I'll work a set amount of hours for you, and you, in turn, will leave my aunt alone and let her conduct business as usual."

He leafed through the portfolio. "I still don't see what's in it for me."

"If after those three months I can convince you of the necessity for her to stay in this spot, you adjust your plans and leave her studio intact. If I can't come up with an alternative to the parking problem, then you can call in your wild card and I will personally help you move in with a smile on my face."

He tapped his fingertips together, calculating the risk, she was sure. "Seems I'd be losing out on time either way. And time is money. Three months is a long time to sit around and wait."

"That's as much time as it'll take to get all the permits squared away and the construction off the ground."

He held her gaze, ignoring the other men in the room. Julia's mouth went dry and her hands felt clammy, but she didn't move, didn't dare look away. She had so much riding on this.

"I'll give you those three months," he finally said. "If you convince me of a profitable alternative, I'll throw in a bonus for you and the studio." He stood and leaned on the desk. "There is one stipulation."

The warning bells went off again. She stood straighter and tilted up her chin. "And what is that?"

"Dance lessons. Private and group during this entire three-month grace period."

"That has nothing to do with this negotiation." Her heart skipped a beat. How could she stay focused on saving the studio if she was sentenced to dance with him, to have space between them swallowed up and their bodies move as one?

"Seriously? I'd think you'd see that as the perfect opportunity to prove me wrong. To show why the studio must go on providing these lessons and deserves to remain intact, as is."

He was right. Dancing was easy. Her aunt was a brilliant dancer and Julia had learned so much from her and was a pretty decent instructor, too. "You're right. Thank you for that opportunity. I'll see what my aunt's schedule looks like."

"Miss Elvira only has to provide the studio. I want you to teach me, darlin', personally."

She swallowed hard. "I don't think that's a good idea."

"Weigh it, Julia. Dance lessons for your three months of prep time that could knock me on my butt, though I doubt it. I think it's a damn fine proposition. What do you think, gentlemen?"

"Damn good deal," Chase said, between mouthfuls of his second pasty.

Francisco stepped toward Julia, uncertainty shadowing his eyes. "You

don't have to agree to anything, Julia."
He slipped his familiar hand over hers.

"You're wrong, Cisco. I'm backed
against a wall. I definitely have to agree
to this, whether I want to or not." She
yanked her hand away.

He nodded, straightened his tie, and
rolled his shoulders. "I never meant
to...I'm sorry. I'll see you Saturday."

She looked at him, her mind a blank.

"I promised your aunt I'd be your
partner to demonstrate a new twist on
the salsa."

"Ah, and we can't have you breaking
promises to my aunt, now, can we?" She
was shocked at her sharp, abrasive tone,
and at the hurt that showed on his face.

They hadn't seen anything yet. "Fine.
For my aunt, anything. Cisco?" She
waited until he faced her. "I'm rounding
up the neighborhood to attend the town
council meeting. We'll protest further
development of the area."

"So be it." He turned stiffly away from
her before she could say anything more.
"Gentlemen, good day."

Despite his stiff posture, he glided from
the room. He had had the same easy
elegance on her aunt's dance floor.

"I want my lessons to start Saturday."
The scowl had returned to Ricardo's face
as he watched Francisco leave the room.

"I have plans, as you've already heard."
He was grating on her nerves, telling her
what to do when she liked to control her
schedule to the T. She would grind her
teeth down to nubs if she hung around
him more than necessary. She jammed
her notepad into her briefcase.

"I'll be there before your group lessons
start."

"Do I have a choice in this?"

He stroked his chin. The silence in the
room was thicker than a courtroom
drama. "Not really, don't you think? You
don't have to make this so difficult for
yourself. Just dance—and prove me
wrong."

"I want this in writing."

"I promised you that already. We don't
have to repeat our gentlemen's
agreements, but for the record, you have
three months to sufficiently prove why I
shouldn't proceed with my already
established plans on buying your aunt's
studio. If you cannot convince me, you
will agree to accept my offer to buy the
studio, since the lease is nearly up
anyway. In the meantime, you will work
ten hours a week on my advertising
campaign. And you will give me two
hours of dance lessons a week."

"Fine." Her ears were ringing and she
had to get out of the line of fire. Suddenly

she felt the pressure of saving her aunt and the studio.

"We'll have the papers drawn up immediately. I can drop them off to you tomorrow, or you can pick them up here when you check in to work."

"Tomorrow? I have other clients, you know."

"I know, and now I'm one of them. I think, darlin', it would be best if you came in two hours a day to start. There's a lot of homework to do initially, and I don't want you overwhelmed. I wouldn't want you burning out before you get a chance to complete my campaign."

"How soon will you be breaking ground?"

"Within the week."

She took a deep breath as she smoothed out her skirt. Business, she could handle. It was Ricardo she wasn't so sure of. "May I take the floor plans and blueprints with me today?" She glanced at her watch, wanting plenty of time to get to her grandfather before he could balk at her offer to take him to the doctor.

"Another appointment?" He placed the floor plans on top of the blueprints and rolled them up together, taking extreme care in rolling them up just so.

"Yes. My grandfather needs..." She shut her mouth. She wouldn't let him see her vulnerable spots. "Yes, I have another appointment."

"Thank you, Julia, for coming in. I know it wasn't easy."

She waited for the sarcasm that never came and swallowed the lump in her throat. "Thank you for accepting my offer. You won't be sorry." She picked up the blueprints, nodded to Chase, and walked out the door.

CHAPTER FIVE

Julia studied the floor plans while Ricardo studied her. Her hair looked shiny and soft and the color of chestnuts at Christmastime. His fingers itched to touch it, to tuck it back behind her ear so that a better glimpse of her neck could be had. Strands fell softly across her cheek, blocking his view of her dark eyes.

That was more than okay. She looked at him with venom these days, even though her voice managed to stay sweet and sultry.

"So, is it salvageable?" He wanted to hear rebuttals and see how her mind worked. He wanted a simple conversation to get them off on the right foot as colleagues. Hell, all he wanted was a second chance to prove his decency.

She glanced up as if she'd forgotten he was there. "Don't patronize me, Montalvo. You know perfectly well all you need is a local angle, something that'll make this restaurant unique to San Diego. I intend to give you that angle."

"I'm sure you'll do a fine job of it. I'm not worried."

She clicked her pen over and over, a faraway look coming into her eyes. "Based on what I've seen, you have a great product. It's not as monstrous as it first looked and if you're intending to keep the style in line with Old Town architectural details, it shouldn't be an eyesore." She popped the pen into the breast pocket of her jacket, a royal blue that made her hair come alive. "Under different circumstances, I'd be thrilled for you."

"You gave me your word you'd give me a hundred percent of your effort." He couldn't take his eyes off her lips, the soft plum color inviting.

"I will." She shrugged. "You realize I'm not doing this for you."

"I know that," he said quietly. "I'm relying on you to make it viable anyway. The faster we get this off the ground and flyin', the faster I'll be out of your hair, one way or another."

She walked over to the window and leaned her forehead against it. He tried to see the studio from her eyes. It looked small and vulnerable when compared to the huge concrete trucks just beyond, the construction company working overtime on pouring the foundation for his restaurant.

He stood behind Julia and wanted to wrap his arms around her slim body and tell her everything would work out fine. He knew from past experience that the churning in his gut signaled otherwise. He struggled to find the right thing to say. "For what it's worth, I wish the circumstances were different, too."

She turned away from the window and looked at him for a long time, with hardly a blink. He wanted to drown in her gaze but realized he probably didn't have a choice. The dark-brown eyes bored deep into him.

Second by second, Julia seemed to peel back layers until he felt she'd gone too far. He shifted his weight, uncomfortable under her scrutiny, afraid of the compassion in her eyes as they searched his face for answers. "There's more to your story, isn't there? To your drive to get this done and head back to Texas?"

He couldn't give her the explanations he knew she wanted to hear. He didn't break eye contact. The silence between them wasn't hostile or volatile, just a common ground, even a respite for a moment. The reason he was doing this boiled down to family, too—only his was at stake as much as Julia's.

Julia moved away, breaking their eye contact. "You wish circumstances could be different? Yes, well, wishes are overrated, aren't they? You know the old children's rhyme—if wishes were fishes, we'd have a fish fry?"

He nodded, not knowing what the hell she was talking about, but not wanting her to go.

"Since you came into my aunt's studio, I've never wished or prayed for anything so hard as I have for you to go away and leave us alone. There wouldn't be any fish left in the sea." She sighed. "Under different circumstances..." She pulled open the door. "Don't be late for your dance lesson."

He let out a deep breath when she closed the door behind her. There was no way he'd let her get to him again. He wasn't a sucker—never had been, never would be—but she had already given him a glimpse of wishful thinking on an entirely different level.

There was no room for emotion in business. But she was right and he'd never admit it—when family was in the middle of business, emotion ruled no matter how hard he tried to tamp it down. He did a good job at fooling everyone so he could get the job done and move on to the next adventure.

He glanced out the window and watched Julia walk across the street with a confident gait. No room for emotion, he repeated.

The irony. Julia *was* emotion. She'd dragged something out of him already, something that didn't belong on the negotiating table. If he wasn't careful, his motto would shatter beyond repair.

He'd worked too long and too hard to get to this position in his life. A little thing like Julia wasn't going to change a damn thing just by throwing some emotion into the already simmering pot.

Julia had almost let her guard down with Montalvo earlier. It wouldn't happen again.

On the dance floor, Ricardo was terrific. The superhero body and cowboy boots should have skidded on the dance floor or tripped over her toes. Instead, he moved silkily, hips and legs in great synchronization. She appreciated every simple movement under her instruction and scrutiny. Only when they put the spotlight on him did he seem to falter.

There was one small problem.

He held her like there was no escaping tomorrow. His palm rested against the small of her back—rather, heated the small of her back. Julia glanced over at the rest of the group in the studio and fought the urge to run to them. There was safety in numbers.

"A dollar for your thoughts." Ricardo pulled back to look at her.

She stopped dancing. "What happened to the infamous penny?"

"They still make them?"

"They're the bartering tool of choice in this neighborhood."

"Your poor pauper-martyr attitude is getting old, Julia. Don't try to be something you're not just to get under my skin." He lifted her chin. "Besides, there are better, more inventive ways of doing that."

She slapped his hand away, shocked at the sensation that rippled through her under his callused fingers. "Ricardo, we have to work on your lack-of-self-esteem problem."

"Not before we work on your manners."

"My, my..." She shoved him away.

He grabbed her before she could take another step. "Control, darlin'," he said through clenched teeth but managed to smile at her anyway. "We made a deal. Now adhere to your end of it. Dancing lessons are buying time for the studio. This lesson isn't done for the day, now, is it?"

He yanked her closer, crushing her body against his.

The breath whipped out of her. She closed her eyes and inhaled slowly, the scent of his cologne seeping through the cotton of his black polo shirt. Was it Stetson? Armani Code? She vaguely remembered working on the Stetson Cologne account years before, but it had never smelled like this on any of the models she'd used. What if he was wearing no cologne at all? If it was all Montalvo?

She slipped her hand out of his and wedged it between them, placing it firmly on his chest. She pushed back the sense of panic that was coursing through her. "It will be over if you don't let me breathe." She felt the slightest give from his hold on her.

"Sorry," he mumbled.

"Proper distance, proper stance." She placed a shaky right hand on his shoulder and took another half step backward until her arm was nearly taut. *Safe,* she thought, her heart rate finally slowing. Lifting her hand, she waited.

He said nothing for a long moment, studying her face. She jutted out her chin a little more and held his gaze, ignoring the way her legs would turn to mush if he continued looking at her like that.

"You play tough, Jule," he finally said and gently slipped his hand around hers. "I'd like my lessons to be an enjoyable experience."

"Normally they would be. But this is business. And there's no room for emotion in business deals. Isn't that your motto?"

"Good memory. Yes, ma'am, that's my motto. That doesn't erase the fact that you feel great under my hand here."

He pressed his hand into the small of her back again, an unbearable heat seeping through her whisper of a dress. "Or that your hair smells like rainwater or that your laugh, the little I've heard of it, sounds like a song. Having you this close makes it enjoyable already, but Lord help me if you ever decide to be civil."

Julia's mouth fell open and she stepped on his toes. Heat climbed to her face. Shame at her behavior tore at her loyalty for her aunt. Her aunt, her grandfather, even her parents would have treated this man more civilly, despite the circumstances.

She glanced at Elvira, a true picture of class and dignity evident in her straight posture, in the way she treated every one of her students and friends. She smiled warmly at her and Ricardo.

Lorenza waved to Julia and gave her the A-OK signal again. Julia looked away quickly. Lorenza, ever the romantic, was so far off base, it wasn't even funny anymore.

Julia was only trying to protect Elvira, to save her business, and conserve a haven for the seniors who lived around her. She looked down at her toes, unsure of what to say to Ricardo. Finally she mustered the courage and met his gaze. "I'm afraid my attitude won't change anytime soon. But you're a quick study. I'd like to think it's due to my tutelage, but I give credit where credit's due. You have the basics down pat, Ricardo. You can join the rest of the class. Perhaps you'll find the conversational stimulation you need there."

She pulled out of his arms, and the coolness against her skin was unwelcome despite the warm afternoon temperatures outside. "Now, if you'll excuse me, I need some fresh air." Walking around the chairs scattered between her and the side door seemed like an obstacle course with no end in sight.

"Mr. Montalvo, please join us." Elvira's voice drifted out to Julia. *How can she do that so effortlessly?* Julia wondered. She glanced back at Ricardo.

The group was waving him over. He looked at them, then at Julia. He

shrugged and ambled to the waiting men
and women.

Ricardo watched her go, the lump in
the pit of his stomach churning like some
alien being had taken over his body. Lord
knew it had already sucked every
semblance of common sense from his
brain.

A blur of fingers waved in front of his
face and the murmur of voices behind him
became clearer. "Hello?"

He looked down at the short woman
standing before him, moving her hand in
an up-and-down motion until he came to.
"Are you deaf, boy?" asked the woman he
already knew as Lorenza.

Before he could answer, she turned to
see where he was looking. A glimpse of
Julia's leg flashed as she stepped from
the room to the brightness of the
outdoors.

"Nope. Not deaf," Lorenza said. "Just
blind."

"Excuse me, ma'am?" He shifted his
gaze to her.

She smiled, the gold lining the edge of
one front tooth distracting him. He was in
for a lecture, he could see it in her eyes,
but there was humor there, along with
compassion. "You two are the most
stubborn young people I've seen in a long

time." She clucked her tongue. "What a waste. Don't let business dictate the desires of your heart."

"My heart has nothing to do with this, ma'am."

"Don't be foolish. Everyone can see the heat between you two."

His heart had nothing to do with it, yet why did it pump louder and harder when Julia re-entered the room?

"And you know the old saying. Your work doesn't keep you warm in bed at night."

He needed to change the course of discussion. He held his arm out to Lorenza. "Would you do me the honor of being my partner on the next round?"

"Of course, Ricardo. I'm no fool—like some people I know."

Elvira clapped her hands. "All right, class, let's get ready." The group formed two circles, the inner one made up of women, with the men standing in a circle directly behind them. "Basic for this song, and we'll switch partners every few minutes."

Julia slipped into her place, as far across the circle from him as possible. She was an incredible sight, lighting the room with her smile. He especially appreciated the short purple velvety dress she wore that flattered her legs. Legs he could imagine wrapped around his body.

He shook his head. *What the hell?*

The group of elderly people surrounded him and had to ground him. Laughing, humming, and swaying, they reminded him of his own family. Their reunions had had the same air about them until his grandmother died two years ago. No one seemed able to get up enough "oomph" to continue organizing the events for the nearly fifty family members. Not even he had taken the initiative. His grandmother would have loved this group and would have loved for him to keep their own family outings going.

Unable to deal with her death and the financial straits his parents had been subjected to, he had run instead. He'd let them down when he was released from the Cowboys, and he intended to make up for it now.

He still cringed at the memory. Before his career as one of the quickest wide receivers had a chance to soar, he'd allowed a little shoulder injury to cause his own demise in the pros. Tackled one too many times until his rotator cuff had had enough and his shoulder had separated, he'd tried to make up for that embarrassment by starting the restaurant chain. It wasn't the same, but he had jumped at the chance, while his name was still recognizable. He hoped people still remembered who he was, who he'd been, if even for a short while.

"If you don't pay attention, son, we're going to leave you in the dust." Julia's grandfather stood to his right. A dapper old gent, Ricardo had liked him from the moment Julia first introduced them. Wizened eyes, like Lorenza's—hell, like all of them in the room—cut him to the quick. There would be no smooth-talking around these guys. They'd already been around the horn more times than they could remember.

"Sir, it's good to see you again."

"Please call me Carlos. Are you getting the hang of this yet, or do you miss that old two-step of yours?"

"Nothing quite like a good, fast two-step."

"Except maybe a woman who can keep up with it." Mischievous eyes met Ricardo's. He waved at the woman in front of them.

Ricardo laughed.

"Julia will give you a run for your money, son."

Ricardo stopped laughing. "Julia," he said, weighing his words carefully, "is one tough cookie. I doubt I could keep up with her."

"So you have noticed her when you two aren't arguing."

"She's hard to miss," he replied before he could stop himself.

The sparkle left the older man's eyes. "We wish you'd leave the studio be, but I understand it's business." He rubbed the center of his chest with gnarled fingers. "We know you'll do what's right in the end."

As if on cue, Elvira quit demonstrating the step and switched on the music. A lively salsa beat filled the air. She clapped in rhythm to it and then shouted, "Positions. Aaaannnd...Go!"

She grabbed Ricardo. Mortified, he fixed his eyes on their feet, trying to count out the rhythm, hoping against hope her toes would be spared. Why was he fine on every other dance floor but here? Forward, quick, quick, slow. Glide back. Quick, quick, slow.

Julia had graciously forgiven his clumsy attempts. But if he physically hurt Elvira by stepping on her feet, an attack from the masses would be inevitable. He concentrated so hard, sweat broke out on his brow.

"Relax, Ricardo." Elvira's voice was commanding but soft. "Let your feet listen to, then follow, the music. If you do two-step, you can do this. Trust yourself." She tapped his shoulder. "Look up, into the eyes. How else will you make that special woman swoon as you sweep her off her feet?"

Elvira twirled out of his arms, leaving him standing alone, with arms outstretched. He slowly brought them to his sides.

"Change partners!" she commanded.

The men in their circle shifted to the right to be standing before a new woman. Julia faced Ricardo.

"Darlin', so we meet again." His heart picked up the fast rhythm, but it didn't have anything to do with the beat. The low-cut V-neck dress might have had something to do with the increased thumping against his ribs.

Julia rolled her eyes. He wanted to yank her chain, get some kind of feisty reaction from her, not this nonchalant annoyance. "Dollar for your thoughts."

"Is this déjà vu?" She stretched her arms out taut so her body would be as far from his as possible. "I hope this is a fast set."

He tugged her in closer to avert his eyes from the gentle curve of her full breasts. They were driving him crazy. "I don't bite, darlin'." He smiled. "Yet."

"You're wrong. You've already sunk your teeth into us and left a gaping wound."

She could just as well have slapped him. His smile evaporated at the venom in her words. "Julia, we've laid a business proposition on the table. Nothing more, nothing less. You're acting like a spoiled child on the verge of a tantrum, not like the professional woman I know you are."

"I'd forgotten how much you know, Ricardo. Puts the rest of us to shame when we let a little emotion trickle into our business dealings."

"That's it." He yanked her against his body, even though the music had stopped. He'd quietly taken her disrespect because he thought he deserved it. But he didn't. He was trying his best to be a gentleman, despite the circumstances.

His blood pressure screamed for mercy around her. "I've tried to come around and give you some leeway. You continually spit that back in my face. You're working for me right now and I demand some kind of mutual respect."

From the corner of his eye he saw Elvira hurriedly jab at her iPod to change the music and fill the heavy silence filling the room. Stunned faces with wide-eyed interest glued their gazes on Julia and him, now at center stage.

"Will you answer me?" he lowered his voice. "Please?"

"Don't demand. I'll try." She sighed deeply. "I promise." Just then she looked over his shoulder, and a smile lit her face. She pushed past him. "Excuse me."

A collective gasp went up around Ricardo. He was left standing alone in the middle of the large, unmoving circle.

"Ricardo!" Lorenza's voice woke him from his stupor. She jerked her head in the direction of Julia's dramatic exit. She started talking animatedly to a group of nearby women. The show had begun.

The music suddenly filled the room but did nothing to change the mood. Everyone looked like cardboard cutouts. Everyone but Julia seemed afraid to move. The music picked up its beat as she reached a clueless Francisco standing at the door.

Francisco looked at her and smiled but immediately took in the surroundings and the somber atmosphere. "Hello everyone." He hesitantly raised his hand in greeting. Only a sprinkling of hands returned the gesture.

"Montalvo?" he asked, nodding his head, a puzzled expression waiting for someone to explain.

Julia glanced back at Montalvo and then slipped her arm into Francisco's and started walking toward the circle.

Another gasp came from the rapt audience.

Elvira called out, "Julia, lessons, *mi amor*." Her worried voice rose above the music.

"Francisco and I are supposed to demonstrate that new twist on the salsa you learned, Auntie." Julia turned and faced Francisco and slipped into his arms, moving to the beat. Francisco had no choice but to follow.

Ricardo crossed the room in several huge strides, each one making Francisco's eyes grow wider. He tapped Julia's shoulder.

She turned to face him. Francisco stepped forward. "She's busy, Montalvo."

"Stay out of this, Valdez," Ricardo growled. He turned to Julia, his fury swirling like an uncontrollable wildfire. "Unacceptable, Julia. We need to talk. Now."

She glanced at the roomful of friends and students. She smoothed her dress, her chest heaving. "Excuse me, Cisco." Then she searched her aunt's face. "I'm sorry, Auntie. I'll be back in a few minutes." She walked out as if it had been her idea in the first place.

Ricardo turned to face the speechless crowd. He bowed slightly from the waist. "If you'll excuse us. I'm sorry for the interruption." And he stormed out of the studio after Julia.

CHAPTER SIX

In silence, they made it to Ricardo's building with no further incident, but the damage had already been done. Entering from the back of the building, they maneuvered through boxes yet to be emptied in the spare room and made their way to his office. He closed the door and leaned against it.

The front reception area was off limits. He'd planned a surprise for Julia. And now he wondered why he'd gone to the trouble.

He looked at her. She rested a hip against the edge of her desk and crossed her arms defiantly. The surprise might not be welcome. Her defiance stirred up his own anger and frustration. Might as well tackle what had brought them there in the first place.

"You're working for me, Julia." Ricardo fixed a stare at her upturned chin, at the plum-colored lips that would have been quivering if they knew the depth of his frustration. "When we're in public, you'll act like you like me."

She stood stock-still, her face calm, her gaze maddening.

"Will you say something?" He pounded his fist on the desktop.

"I'm not that good an actress."

"Damn it, Julia. Stop fighting me on this. You of all people should know that image is everything in this business. You *will* paint a pretty picture of me and my restaurants around your aunt's clientele. If you continue to sabotage my work, I'll renege on my half of the deal. Your three months' grace period will end right this minute if you don't promise me full cooperation."

"You're right. You're absolutely right. You'll have my full cooperation." She stood, ready to leave. "Will that be all— *Boss?*"

He raked his fingers through his hair, ready to yank it out by the handfuls. "No." He stalked over to her. "It doesn't have to be like this, Julia. Work with me, please. Be nice, for chrissakes." *Nice? What had she reduced him to? Nice and emotion had nothing to do with the business at hand.*

He was trying, damn it. Didn't she see that?

"I can't," she said quietly and sat back on the edge of the desk.

"You can, darlin'." He stood before her and pulled her to her feet.

She shook her head slowly. "You bring out the beast in me. The worst in me."

Her hands were softer than he ever imagined. Tough façade. Tender when you broke through. "I'd like to think I bring out that protective streak in you. Mama bear protecting her baby cubs, so to speak. Your aunt is lucky she has you."

She studied his face. He let her. The silence grew heavy, but not uncomfortable. "You scare me sometimes," she said finally, but without a hint of fear.

"I don't mean to. Honest." He bent and touched his lips to hers.

Her eyes grew wide, wider than he'd seen. He didn't release her. She didn't push him away.

His arms automatically encircled her, wanting to protect her.

Her lips were incredibly soft. His mouth tingled like some four-alarm chili had taken root there. He wanted his mouth to veer from those lips, to travel the length of her neck, to her earlobe, her cheek, but his common sense kicked in. If his lips left hers, she'd make a run for it. He wasn't ready to let her go.

For a second he thought it his imagination, then he was sure of it. Her lips parted slightly, as if taking a shallow breath, softened even more, and she closed her eyes. He deepened the kiss, wanting to savor that mouth and drown out the arguments that had reduced him to monster status.

Her grip on his shirt loosened. She laid one hand on the back of his neck and pulled him closer. Her other hand stroked his cheek and singed his skin, the tender touch of her fingers as violent as any explosive.

A moan soared up between them. He let his hand fall from her hair and make its way down her back, each inch of her body burning his hand like flickering flames.

She rose to her tiptoes, and her full breasts rubbed against his chest. The velvety dress was a flimsy shield against his body.

He held her close but was unable to get close enough to this woman who'd turned his world upside down and dragged her family in to watch. He didn't give a damn.

Right now, he'd stand on his head for them, promise them shares in the restaurant chain, throw a fiesta like they'd never seen. Just as long as Julia stayed in his arms and kept her mouth on his for a few minutes, the horrendous monster she'd made him out to be might disappear.

The room grew stifling hot. At worst, her clothes might stick to the curves of her body and he'd have to help pry them off her. At best, their arguments would melt on their tongues like chips of ice on a wicked summer day in south Texas.

His fingers trailed along her torso, feeling the edge of her full breasts, and she sucked in her breath, breaking their kiss. She looked at him with desire in her eyes—there was no mistaking that, no way to hide the reactions of their traitorous bodies. He brought a hand up to her cheek and brushed back the strand of hair clinging there. She covered his hand with hers.

"Julia, darlin'," he whispered, his voice no more than a croak. "Why do you fight me so?" He twined his fingers with her delicate soft ones.

Tears welled up in her eyes. "You know why. You put me between a rock and hard place, Montalvo."

"I'm sorry. I, I..." He didn't know what else to say. Not when her skin felt like this, not when her body molded itself to his, not when her lips looked swollen, not when she was this close to crying.

She managed to smile. "Speechless? That must be a first."

He placed his finger on her lips. "We have to work on your idea of sweet nothings."

"Like I said, you bring out the worst of me, Montalvo."

"And the best." Again, he leaned down and touched his lips to hers. *Man...heaven.*

A bell jingled somewhere in the back of his mind. A warm gust of wind swirled around them, shaking loose some flowery scent. "Do you smell that?" he whispered in her ear, afraid only he could smell it.

"Mmm-hmm. Lilies."

"Good," he said, relieved. "I like your perfume even better than that." He nuzzled her ear, her neck, her jaw.

"I'm not wearing any." Her voice sounded far away.

"All you?" He was truly fascinated. "If I could bottle that up, we'd make a killing." He kissed her again. "No. I'd rather die a poor man—I wouldn't want to share it with anyone."

"Spoken like a true entrepreneur." She stood on her tiptoes and pressed her body against him, knowing exactly the effect she had on him. He let her take the reins, knowing their chemistry ignited more than passion. She definitely had an unfair advantage.

A knock sounded on the closed door that separated the office from the reception area. They jumped out of each other's arms.

The door swung open. Chase and Francisco stood in the doorway.

Chase had the silliest-looking grin on his face Ricardo had ever seen. Francisco, on the other hand, looked as if his face would crumble into thousands of pieces, like a boulder falling from a mountaintop to shatter on the earth below.

Ricardo focused on Chase, couldn't bring himself to look at Julia, and didn't want to spoil the euphoria by confronting Francisco. "What's up, Chase?"

"We're all waiting, dude."

Julia stepped toward the credenza where she'd left her briefcase before the dance lessons. "All?"

Ricardo turned to look at her and immediately regretted it. Julia definitely had that Helen of Troy magic about her. She could launch a war with that face. He could perish. He wiped the back of his hand against his throbbing mouth.

Chase took a sip of whatever was in the Styrofoam cup he held. It looked mighty refreshing to Ricardo, his parched throat needing relief.

"Your family, neighbors. Everybody's outside. They came directly from their dance lessons. I have all the food and drink set up. We're just waiting for a grand entrance."

Color drained from Julia's face. She glanced at her watch. "What are you talking about?"

"Rick's open house."

"Open house? What for?" A wary look came into her eyes.

The Julia he'd had the opportunity to see was gone. His stomach sank.

"Don't let your dark thoughts think the worst of me, Julia. No bribes. They came of their own accord. No one gave me a welcome party to the neighborhood, so I thought I'd throw an open house, let people come and not be afraid to ask me questions. I knew you wouldn't feel comfortable helping me on this, so I planned it myself. With Chase's help."

She touched his arm, but it did little more than send a ripple of electricity over his body. "I think you *conveniently* forgot to tell me. How could you?" Her mouth set into that grim line again as she walked past him. He realized how much he wanted to see her smile. Make her smile.

Ricardo touched her arm. "It was a gesture of goodwill. I want to do the right thing." He leaned down and whispered in her ear, "If you want to freshen up before you go out there, you can use my bathroom."

She started to say something but shut her mouth. She ran her hand through her hair. "Thank you."

When she shut the door behind her, Chase laid into him. "Working on intensive advertising strategies for the restaurant?" He walked over to the desk and started tossing the paperweight between his hands.

Francisco leaned on the doorjamb like a model posing for a *GQ* shot. "You know, Montalvo, you're already walking a thin line in this neighborhood. I wouldn't do anything to make you tip to the other side."

"Excuse me?"

"Julia is family here. You're an outsider. Your actions could look like you're using her. I'd be careful how you treat her and her family if you want any kind of support from me or the community with your project. She's already a formidable foe for you. You don't need bad publicity."

"Then she's *your* formidable foe, as well, isn't that right, Valdez? Or have you forgotten how much I've sunk into your campaign with the agreement of your unquestionable support?"

Francisco straightened his tie and shrugged his shoulders. "Don't play games with me, Montalvo. Your support is appreciated, but I can make you or break you in this neighborhood."

"I can say the same for you." Ricardo cracked his knuckles, an easy way to divert his negative energies.

Even though they stood well enough away from each other, Chase planted his body between them. "It's not about the two of you. The faster you see that, the faster you'll get the community support you both want. I doubt either of you will get Julia's support at this rate."

Ricardo glanced at the closed bathroom door. How badly did he want that restaurant? Julia in his arms had given him a glimpse of ... something. It seemed worth more than an infinite number of restaurants. The realization frightened Ricardo. But then he thought that he couldn't stop, that he had to have more than enough restaurants to ensure his mom and dad, his family, would be well taken care of the rest of their lives.

Julia stepped through the doorway and stared at each of them, starting and ending with Ricardo. "I missed something important, didn't I?"

"Ask me anything, Julia," Ricardo said, "and I'll give you an answer."

"Good. I'll hold you to that." She walked past all of them, and straight into the front office.

"Julia!" Her name seemed to echo a hundred times over.

Ricardo could see even from where he stood that she hunched her shoulders as if she were being pelted by snowballs. Only for a moment. She waved to the crowd. "Hey, everybody."

Ricardo was impressed. Nothing like being thrust into a surprise situation and turning it in your favor.

She ducked back into Ricardo's office. "My entire family's out there," she hissed. "The entire neighborhood, everybody. The room's jammed."

"Is there anyone I haven't met?"

"Don't Montalvo." She turned to Chase. "How long have you all been out there?"

"Fifteen minutes?"

"Oh, no." Julia covered her face with her hands. "I've been consorting with the enemy. They're going to know instantly."

"Know what, Julia?" Chase asked innocently.

Julia ignored him and began smoothing her dress.

Her slender fingers mesmerized Ricardo. Could something that delicate be so lethal, weakening him with a touch?

Francisco looked at Ricardo with disgust, even though he responded to Julia's comment. "Yes. You're in enemy territory with no real backup."

"You're a part of this too, Cisco." She stopped fiddling, planted her hands on her hips, and turned to Ricardo. "I know you're trying to buy the business, but can you stop trying to befriend them? Are you using them to get to me?"

She paced. "Don't drag them into this more than you already have, especially if you're going to hurt them in the process and then just leave them in the dust. You won't be here to see the effects after the dust settles. By then you'll be long gone."

He wondered who exactly she was talking about, wondered if she lumped herself in there with the rest of the clan. He wouldn't go there. "You think I'm using them to get to you? That's rich, darlin'. You don't have an ego problem either, do you?" He smiled.

"It's not my ego I'm worried about, Ricardo. I can take anything you dish out, but my family shouldn't be subjected to any of your so called business strategies just to have the rug pulled out from beneath them when the timing's right."

"Geez, darlin', I thought we'd worked through all that. Don't you trust me yet?"

"I have no reason to trust you. You didn't even mention something as simple, yet monumental, as this event to me."

"Jule, there's a sign in the window about the open house, for cryin' out loud. Give me a break."

"There is?" She stalked past them and they followed. The crowd parted to let them through.

She turned to face the building. The crowd waited silently. She walked back in. "There's a sign, all right. Sorry. I never saw it. I sometimes jump to conclusions."

"Sometimes?" His sarcasm was lost on her. Or perhaps she just ignored him. Either way, she had ammo and he was her target.

Julia waved over a good-looking couple. "Mom, Dad, come here a minute. There's someone I want you to meet."

Julia grabbed Ricardo's forearm and pulled him close to her side. "Mom and Dad, this is Ricardo Montalvo, owner of a chain of restaurants including the one going up here—*The Ranch in Old Town*. He's also one of my clients, temporarily."

"Oh, *mija*, we've already met." A big man himself, her father shook Ricardo's hand in earnest. "Matter of fact, he helped me unload the newest shipment of art and whipped up some margaritas afterward that were the best I'd had in a long time. Reminded me of the ones I used to make."

"Secret Texas ingredient that gives them that extra punch." Ricardo rocked back on his heels just like her father. They mumbled some incoherent things to each other and chuckled.

Her smile vanished. "You've already met?" She glared at Ricardo. What was he doing, infiltrating her life and befriending her family? Why did it feel like she was slipping into quicksand around him?

Her mother smiled, and the radiance rose to her hazel eyes. She shook Ricardo's outstretched hand, the contrast of his dark skin beautiful against hers, so fair. "He brought over some coffee and *pan dulce* the other morning and we visited for a while," her mother said.

"Of course he did."

"Are you all right, *mija?* You don't look well." She felt Julia's forehead with cool fingers.

"Let me see, Mrs. Rios." Ricardo touched his hand to Julia's forehead, then let it slide down her cheek. "She does seem a little warm to me, too."

"Stop talking about me in the third person." She smiled sweetly. "I'm just fine, Mom. Montalvo makes my blood boil, that's all. Not very good for my health, I'm afraid."

"When you're on a mission, everyone makes your blood boil." Her mother patted her cheek. "You have to ease up." She waved to Aunt Elvira on the other side of the room. "Try to enjoy the party, Julia." She kissed Julia and hurried off. Her father gave Julia's shoulder a squeeze and slapped Ricardo on the back before ambling off behind her.

"Good to know I'm not the only one you treat this way. Do I make your blood boil beyond business?"

Julia shivered. If he only knew. And he wouldn't. She'd lost control in a moment of weakness. She leaned over so that only Ricardo could hear her. "Stop inching your way into our lives. I don't want anyone else to get hurt." He frightened her. What he made her feel frightened her even more. It had nothing to do with open houses or business tactics.

"I feel right at home here and I'll do everything in my power to try to belong and make everyone happy in the process. It's what I do best."

She fixed her gaze on him. "Don't even go there, Montalvo. What you do best is uproot families and try to squeeze in before blindsiding them and taking over their businesses and communities. End of story."

What he did best was kiss her so remarkably, he made her lose her footing. Made her mission blur. He made the war she waged seem futile, made her question what they were fighting about in the first place. She couldn't lose sight of what she had to do because one little kiss had melted the icy façade she tried so hard to hide behind.

She clapped her hands. "Everyone, thank you for coming. Let's offer Ricardo Montalvo a great big welcome." Everyone followed her lead and clapped and whistled a greeting. "Thank you for opening your office to us today and offering us all this wonderful food and the promise of a good time."

Another round of applause filled the room. Every imaginable space was filled with platters of appetizers: homemade nachos and slices of jicama and carrots to accompany the salsa and dips. Enchiladas and tacos, rice and beans, sangria and margaritas and virgin drinks were set up at a table at the far wall.

"Make sure you introduce yourselves to him so that he can put real live faces to the businesses here in Old Town, so that he can see there's more to our businesses than our storefronts. Now eat and enjoy.

We'll see you at the town council meeting on Monday."

She turned to Elvira. "Auntie, could you do what you do best?"

Elvira waved to her, then flipped on the switch of Ricardo's iPod as if she'd been using it for years. Francisco eased into position next to Julia and her parents. Julia sighed and looked at Ricardo across the room until his gaze met hers. Music filled the air and for a moment, Julia thought that Ricardo could very easily fit in here and like it if he gave it half a chance.

Ricardo started toward Francisco, ready to wipe the smug look from his face. A hand clamped over his forearm. Looking a bit frail, Don Carlos didn't allow that to loosen his grip.

"You don't want to do that, son. Francisco's been in the family since he was in diapers."

"He's dangerous," Ricardo growled.

"Not really," said Don Carlos. "But he's mighty protective, and like Julia, quite emotional about what matters. It clouds their vision sometimes."

"Is he still in love with her?" Ricardo saw the way Francisco had looked at Julia earlier and it had thrown him off.

"Wouldn't doubt it."

"Is Julia still in love with him?" Suddenly, that's what mattered more.

"No. Not in the way you're thinking, but you should ask her directly." Don Carlos rubbed his chest, a faraway smile lighting his eyes. "There could be worse things."

"Like what?"

"Letting opportunities slip through your fingers like silky strands of hair. Or seeing with your eyes instead of your heart. Or not understanding that business is only a small part of life."

"Business sustains us. Leaves a legacy. Helps provide for those we love." Who was he trying to sell the idea to? Don Carlos or to himself? "Tell me. Is Julia always good at pushing people away who want to help her?"

"I'm afraid so. Especially since she doesn't see it as helping. Her interpretation is much different than yours. And she wants to be the one to help, the one with all the answers, the one to protect us older folks." He let go of Ricardo's arm and patted his shoulder. "But she has to learn that giving in a little is not giving up."

"I'm afraid it is where I'm concerned."

"Then change her mind." Don Carlos walked away, shaking his head. "And it wouldn't hurt to impress her at the town council meeting."

Ricardo took a swig of his drink. That would be easier said than done.

The air in the small meeting room at the town hall grew stifling. Ricardo and Julia stood at the front near the councilmen, a hot breath away from the neighbors jammed into the first row of seats.

Francisco rapped the gavel and ordered the meeting to come to order. The bright lights of the cameras from the television news crew focused on him. "Thank you all for coming to this impromptu meeting." He straightened and gripped the sides of the lectern. "I'm always very happy to see so much support and involvement from this community. As always, I'm honored to represent you."

The crowd clapped. Relief spread over Julia. She and Francisco had lived here all their lives. This clan, so much like family, wasn't going to allow Ricardo Montalvo to squeeze into the neighborhood and flatten her aunt's studio.

"We have only one item on the agenda. We are, simply, officially welcoming a new businessman to the area. Many of you have already had the opportunity to meet." He adjusted his burgundy tie, a splash of color against the crisp white shirt and navy suit he wore. "I'd like to hand the mic over to Mr. Ricardo Montalvo so that he can tell us a little about himself and his plans."

Smooth move, thought Julia. Francisco stepped back to let Ricardo take the heat. After Ricardo explained his intentions, Francisco would gauge the audience reaction. That would determine how to tell them he was supporting Ricardo's project.

She had to think they wouldn't get to that point. She could see the crowd now, up in arms, angry at Ricardo's assumptions and invasion. They would run him out of town to come to Elvira's rescue. Her heart leapt. He'd invaded her life too, and if she were honest with herself, had to admit that he'd brought in passion and made her feel alive outside of business and negotiations, advertising campaigns and missions.

Ricardo took the microphone from its perch. "This feels like home."

Julia rolled her eyes. Then again. There was no room for another politician in the neighborhood. He was at ease with the mic in his hand. Julia suddenly hoped he wasn't also into karaoke. She glanced around. He'd have them in the palm of his hand.

"I'm opening a sports theme restaurant and dance club, right between Miss Elvira's studio and the shop that specializes in hand-painted signs." He stepped around the lectern and walked down the cramped center aisle. "Although I'm open to changing the theme of the restaurant if that will help me fit in better."

A soft wave of murmurs washed through the room.

He held up one hand. "Not to be alarmed, folks. The lovely Julia Rios has graciously offered to help me with an ad campaign. The restaurant will be a positive addition to the neighborhood, and we'll keep you updated on the project. You are more than welcome to visit me on the worksite or in my office across the street from Miss Elvira's with any questions you may have."

He made eye contact with as many people in as many rows as he could. If he were anyone else, Julia would have been impressed with the way he worked the crowd.

"I do want to make it clear that change in the neighborhood may be inevitable, but we'll wait for three months to see if we can implement Julia's suggestions at that time." He touched his fingers to his forehead in a simple salute, aimed at Julia. "If her suggestions are viable, we'll leave the rest of the block untouched by the project."

He made his way back to the makeshift stage. "In the meantime, I look forward to working closely with Julia and getting to know each of you over the summer. Old Town seems like the best place to live and work, and I'm looking forward to being a part of it."

The crowd started a tentative clap, but when Francisco joined in, they didn't hold back—the clapping becoming thunderous. Ricardo replaced the microphone, waved, and took his place near Julia again.

Julia fumed at both men. She'd been set up.

"Thank you, Mr. Montalvo." Francisco spoke boldly into the microphone. "I'm sure you'll find this the best place in San Diego for your restaurant. Please call on me or any of us if we can be of service. Thank you, everyone, for coming today."

Lorenza threaded her way to Ricardo and Julia. "Finally we learn why you're really here. It will be a great pleasure to have you in the neighborhood. We always like news—I mean, new neighbors, of course. Will you be taking any more dance lessons?" She glanced at Julia, trying to appear innocent but failing miserably.

"As a matter of fact, I will." He put his arm around Julia like they were buddies. "Julia's offered to teach me more salsa over the summer."

Julia shrugged off his arm. "I made a deal with the devil," she muttered.

Ricardo leaned down and whispered, his breath warm in her ear, "You better get to work. The neighborhood's depending on you." He reached into his pants pocket and pulled out a silver key on the end of an "I Love Texas" key chain. "And to make things really official, my office is your office. It'll be my pleasure to see you there every day."

She stared him square in the eye. "It's going to be a hell of a long summer."

He laughed that rich, wonderful laugh and sauntered off, his jeans just right on his long legs and tight butt. He shook countless hands along the way to the door. The women watched him appreciatively; the men slapped him on the back and laughed at his jokes.

And Julia swallowed hard. Correction. It was going to be one hell of a long hot, hot summer.

CHAPTER SEVEN

The music, as it had in the past weeks, lured Ricardo to the studio. He hadn't been as productive as his agenda had called for, but the trade-offs had been worth it.

Julia stood in position with one very embarrassed young man. Every other seat was filled with fidgeting boys and girls he figured to be about twelve years old, and their taunting of the poor victim was relentless.

"Music," called Julia. Once the music started, the class quieted down and watched with great interest. As the boy's feet fell into an easy beat, he looked up at Julia with a beaming face.

Ricardo clapped at the end of the song. The surprise on Julia's face pleased him. He sauntered into the room. "What's with the half pints?"

"Half pints?" The words echoed through the room, the energy bristling.

"Our pro bono. They're on year-round school schedules and it gets a little boring. So we teach classes to sixth-graders twice a week, rotating to different schools in the area."

"Sixth grade?"

"It's a pivotal age. Beside, they're the future for our music. We want them to appreciate it, love it, make it a part of their lives as they grow up." She wiped her hands together as if she were ridding them of sticky crumbs. "We're lucky. Dancing is making a comeback right now. As long as I mix it up, they've stayed interested."

"Why wouldn't they?" Ricardo took a good look at the group. They stared back at him in stony silence, wary and typical sixth-graders. "Why sixth grade?" he asked, loud enough that they could hear every word. "I know from experience that sixth-graders are disrespectful and difficult to teach. Do they have any talent? Can they dance?"

"Hey!" A murmur went up from the crowd.

Julia quieted them down. "Ricardo, they were perfectly fine until you came stirring things up again. You to do that well, leaving devastation in your wake like some wayward tornado."

He ignored her and turned to the class. "Is she a good teacher?" He jerked his thumb at Julia.

An enthusiastic nod came from the crowd, then quickly turned to a more subdued one. They all leaned forward in their seats.

He leaned in conspiratorially. "Ms. Rios won a lot of awards for her salsa and cumbia dancing back in the day. You guys are lucky to have her. Don't take her for granted."

Heat rose to her face. "Thanks, Ricardo. Trying to start a mutiny?"

He held his hands up. "Who, me?"

She stepped forward and patted the young boy's shoulder, indicating that he could go. "Because Mr. Montalvo is my advanced student and Miss Elvira couldn't be here today, he's going to help out the last half hour." She grabbed his hand.

More catcalls sounded.

"Wait a minute." Ricardo had been blindsided.

"Everyone come up and form a circle around us. We'll go through the basic step again. Hurry now. Time's wasting."

"You can't be serious, darlin'." Ricardo tried to pull away, but she held firmly. "You don't know who you're dealing with, honey. Two can play your game."

She called for music and stood in position before him. He reluctantly took her in his arms, the kids' taunting growing louder. He dropped his hands and commanded, "Everyone get a partner. If I have to do this, so do you."

Julia looked at him, amused. "Now, now, patience with the children."

He looked down, took a deep breath, then took her in his arms. Now this felt right. "Patience is my middle name, darlin'." He had to forget his legs felt like Jello around her and pull out all the stops. He used to be smooth on the dance floor. Of course he was smooth on the dance floor. He could do it again.

"Mmm-hmm." She turned to the kids, watching the goofy looks on their faces. "Everyone have a partner? Okay, watch me and Mr. Montalvo first."

The music started and Ricardo stepped on her foot. The kids howled with laughter. Ricardo was not enjoying the spotlight.

Julia obviously was. She laughed along with them.

She glanced around. "Kids. They'll eat you alive." She cocked her head, studying him. "So, there is a way to intimidate you." She started the silky movement again. "Look in my eyes, Ricardo. Trust yourself."

"Yes, teacher." Ricardo decided to give her a taste of her own medicine. He looked deep into her eyes. They grew wider when he didn't look away. Her mouth parted slightly but remained blessedly silent. And then she tripped on his toe.

The kids howled again, and a soft red blush crept up Julia's neck.

"Ruthless, aren't they?" To run his mouth up that neck and follow the trail of her blush, to her earlobe, up to her temple, across her cheek, to her inviting lips, he'd endure the kids as long as it took, then send them across the street for some *pan dulce* to keep them occupied for a while.

"Revenge doesn't suit you, Ricardo. You're no monster." She lifted her chin in that maddening way of hers and started that wicked sway.

She finally noticed—and admitted he wasn't a monster. Suddenly his apprehension melted away as he felt her body against his. His hand in hers. All the moves she'd taught him the last few weeks became as natural as breathing. He took the lead.

"Ah, honey, revenge wasn't what I had in mind." Surprise registered in her eyes, but only for a moment. Then a smile crept up and looked radiant as she gave in and followed his lead. The music filled the room, the kids watched in silence, and he watched her with what probably was that goofy look Chase always referred to.

Lord help him, but her moves were sultry and confident and made him want to sweep her off her feet. He threw himself in the rhythm, forgetting his self-consciousness. That bit of confidence was back. He threw in the half body turn, the spin, the cross body lead.

And she kept up, smooth as silk. Damn but he liked the way her body responded to his. He faltered. Afraid to step on her toes, he watched her feet.

"Don't," she whispered. "Look up. Look in my eyes. You got it."

He nodded and looked up. But the way she held his gaze reduced his moves to auto pilot. He didn't want to break the eye contact, the body contact. He could look at her all day and then some.

"Let's ditch the kids, Julia," he whispered in her ear, his words slurring after drinking her in like exquisite champagne.

"We can't do that!"

Her reaction made him think that perhaps she would consider it.

She firmly pulled her hand out of his. Ah. The logical Julia was back. Head over heart with this one. Maybe he just wanted her to relent, just a little bit, to show that he wasn't the only one willing to let business fall by the wayside.

"Better get used to the kids," she said. "I'm hiring a couple to help me in your office."

"You can't do that."

"Sure I can."

To have twelve-year-olds underfoot, warily criticizing him, defiant in their own right. He already had enough of that from Julia. What he didn't want was another obstacle coming between him and her. He just wanted to get to know her better. "What about that image we talked about?"

"They'll improve it. They need business exposure. You need exposure to manners and patience. I need help with my deadline, fast approaching. You're going to love my work and end up leaving my aunt alone."

She patted his chest. If he tore opn his shirt, he would surely see her palm print branded there.

"Besides," she said, "you need to be intimidated once in a while. It's good for you."

She turned to the group and pulled over a couple to stand next to her. "Mr. Montalvo will now dance with Patricia while I dance with Jimmy."

Ricardo's mouth dropped open. Wait until he got her on his turf. Business reigned there, not kids, and certainly not Julia. Here he felt like the Wicked Witch of the West, melting, melting.

He glanced at her curvaceous body and swallowed hard. He'd have to admit, he wasn't putting up much resistance to her heat and the threat of melting these days. Sweet Jesus, but she brought on the sleepless nights with bouts of passionate, free-falling fantasy.

He wanted to seduce her without distractions. He wanted to run warm hands over her body like an artist, working it. Appreciating every curve, every smooth length of skin, every rise and fall of shuddering breath. With his hands, his lips, his heat, her body would eventually loosen under his touch until it molded perfectly against his. He stretched out the collar of his polo shirt.

He sauntered over to the folding chair where he'd left his Stetson, put it on and walked back over to the center of the room. The hat gave him an added dose of testosterone. Now he could handle anything she dished out.

He forced himself to listen to Julia's instructions. She had the kids' rapt attention. He was impressed. Maybe sixth-graders weren't as intimidating as they were made out to be. Then again, they looked as smitten with her as he was. No wonder they were listening. He rocked back, quite enjoying the show.

Julia dismissed the group into couples again. The little girl next to him tugged on his sleeve.

Ricardo tipped his hat to the girl and offered his arm to her. "May I have this dance?"

She giggled and held onto his forearm. They all danced until the bus came to pick them up.

Their laughter and high-fives put Ricardo on cloud nine. "That felt good," he said as he folded up the chairs and stacked them against the wall. "They weren't the terrors I feared they would be."

"Nor were you. You're human after all."

"Don't be so sure, darlin'. You just caught me with my pants—my guard down."

She sashayed her way over to him. He stopped working just because he enjoyed watching her move.

"You're nice when you're not ruthless, Ricardo. You should try it more often."

"I'm not ruthless, darlin', I'm just a damn good businessman. If you took off those blinders of yours, you'd see me for what I am, maybe even appreciate what you saw."

"I see you shift back and forth like Jekyll and Hyde and wonder who the real Ricardo is."

"It's all me, Julia. The good and the bad, like anybody else."

She sighed and smiled. "Thanks for helping me today. You were a good sport. I'm sure the kids will be talking about it for days and you'll be famous for a while."

He grabbed her hand and twirled her around, then pulled her close to him. He kissed her on the cheek. "Thank you. I actually had a good time after they stopped laughing at me."

She laughed. "They do tend to humble you. You did great with them, though, and with your dancing. It's a matter of trusting yourself, Ricardo, and giving yourself over to the beat."

He wanted to give himself over to her—and not just on the dance floor. "I have a great instructor. I'll keep practicing. Promise."

She pulled away from their embrace. "I'll see you tomorrow. It's time to put my nose to the grindstone. I only have a few weeks until the advertising campaign is due." She reached the side door and lifted her hand with a hesitant wave. "Lock up on your way out."

Ricardo raised his hand to his face and inhaled Julia. He wiped it across his chest, knowing her scent and feel would surface in those fitful dreams.

Her words rang in his ears as he shut the door behind him. He didn't trust himself around her at all anymore and didn't like that feeling one bit. He'd given himself over, all right, and it wasn't to the beat that came from any salsa rhythm.

Julia held her breath as Ricardo looked over the preliminary advertising presentations she'd prepared. The last couple of days she'd been glued to her work, hoping upon hope to find a way to impress him and convince himself to leave the studio intact. She'd been meticulous, so now it was up to her presentation and his interpretation of her campaign proposal.

Why on God's green earth did she worry about his opinion? But she knew the answer before the question had fully formed. She saw herself in every line she'd drawn, in every word she'd tweaked to get the advertising message across the best way possible.

Her work was an extension of herself; her creativity flowed and she poured a little of her heart and soul into every client's work she believed in. That included Montalvo's project.

Which was a startling revelation for her. Montalvo had a wonderful product. If he'd been attempting to develop it anywhere else in San Diego, she would have supported him wholeheartedly.

"These are some of the best I've seen, darlin'." He scrolled through the PowerPoint and set aside the detailed step-by-step, timed agenda for the advertising campaign. "Where have you been all my life?" he asked without looking up.

She brought her hand to her throat, uncertainty washing over her like the heavenly scent of roses, lilies, and jasmine tinging the air around them. *Fool,* she thought, when she came to her senses. Thinking that even for a second his comment could have meant anything more than referring to her as a professional colleague was ludicrous.

"Well, Montalvo, a wise man once said, what matters is the here and now. I take it you're happy with my proposals?"

"I'm ecstatic, darlin'."

"Wow. Don't hold back." She came around the desk to peer over his shoulder for a better view. She took a deep breath. "The ad campaign has been easy to work with. You have a great product. If you like this, I hope you'll be open to the alternatives I've been working on that would keep the studio intact."

She leaned over him and pointed to one frame, her breasts pressing dangerously against his arm. "The alternatives are a spin-off of this." Pulling away, her breasts scraped against his warm and sturdy body, making heat whip through her like a flame come to life.

He cleared his throat. "I look forward to seeing them if they're anything like these samples of your work."

He turned his head and stared at her. Their faces were only inches apart. A breath away from heaven. She could smell his minty toothpaste, could see the hint of five o'clock shadow emerging, could easily have leaned in another inch and kissed his mouth, a mouth that had invoked sweet dreams into the last few restless nights.

She turned and moved several steps away from him, afraid he could read her mind and see in her eyes the desire that had flamed there since the first time they'd kissed. "I'm sorry. I didn't mean to touch you like that. It was just a...a..." She stopped digging herself deeper into the hole she'd dug and planted her hands on her hips. "You're enjoying this, aren't you?"

"Very much." He straightened and sauntered over to her, took her by the hand, and pulled her close to him.

"This really isn't a good idea, Ricardo." Then why, pray tell, were her feet not listening to her words and running out the door?

"What are you afraid of, Julia?"

A strangled noise came from her throat. "Nothing," she managed and backed up a little. "Everything. There's so much at stake."

"Suit yourself. I'll respond to your earlier comment, then."

"Which was?"

"Don't hold back." He reached over and flipped on the iPod. Raising the volume to deafening levels allowed Shakira to belt out her latest dance music.

"Are you crazy?"

"Just for you." He smiled wide and chucked her on the chin. "I mean, your work, darlin', your work. We've got a winner!"

He let out a raucous yell, grabbed his Stetson off the desk and tossed it into the air. He grabbed Julia and lifted her off the ground, dancing his way around the room, carrying her with ease.

She squirmed for no more than a few seconds before giving in. She wrapped her arms around his neck and leaned her head far back, filled with exhilaration.

"We're on our way, baby! You, darlin', are the most talented advertising exec I've ever seen. You're an angel in disguise." He placed her on the floor. "Damn good disguise, I might add." He looked at her appreciatively.

"Flattery will get you nowhere, Montalvo—not with me." Strong words for her weak-kneed response anytime Ricardo happened to be within arm's distance lately.

"All right, then, darlin'. Let's celebrate instead." He wanted to do something special, take her away from the safety of his office.

She laughed, a beautiful, welcoming sound he didn't hear often enough. He wanted to think she was getting comfortable enough around him to be herself and stop being so defensive. He stared at the creamy skin, at the lips he knew were softer and more tender than should be legally allowed, and touched her cheek.

"Montalvo?" She sobered and snapped her fingers in front of his face. "Snap out of it."

"Am I a slave driver? You've been working too hard."

"I love my work. You're not a slave driver. You just want the job done the right way. The bottom line, though, is that saving my aunt's studio is my ultimate goal. That keeps me focused." She grabbed her tablet and placed it in her briefcase. "As much as I've come to enjoy working for you, I don't ever forget it. I will always defend my aunt, my parents, and my family first. A stellar campaign will make you see that there are always alternatives."

"Julia, I…" How could he tell her he'd been wrong, at least wrong in the way he'd pushed her against the wall and panicked her family? "I've learned something from you, too, believe it or not."

"Is that a hard pill to swallow?" She looked at him for a moment and boldly touched her hand to his cheek, wondering if he felt anything she did. She couldn't make assumptions.

She dropped her hand from his cheek and the warmth went with it. He picked up her hand and rubbed his thumb over the back of it. More warmth Julia didn't want to give up just yet.

There's no room for emotion in business rang through his head, yet he looked at Julia and knew they were on the same page, that perhaps she'd stop judging him. "I'd go to any lengths to protect my family, too. I need to do this. To do the right thing for them—and for your family. I promise I'm trying to find a way." Or maybe she'd just see the weak link, that he was very much being driven by emotion.

She hesitated for only a second, a look of doubt coming into the dark-brown eyes that lured him into uncharted territory. "I believe you, Ricardo," she said quietly.

All he could do was nod. "Then we understand each other." He refrained from touching her hair, enjoying the way a thick strand was perfectly cut to frame the oval shape of her face. "Let me take you to the restaurant that sparked the idea for my chain. Maybe it'll give you better insight for the advertising campaign. Food's good, too."

"Will you tell me your life story on the way?"

"Nah. I really want you awake—it's the only way to appreciate the sights, the details, the magic of the place. Can you be ready in an hour?"

"Of course."

"I'll pick you up then. Dress comfortably and bring a change of clothes for a night on the town. It's a bumpy ride 'til we get there. I'll make it a night you won't forget."

"I wouldn't expect anything less from you." She shook her head and headed for the door. With her hand on the doorknob, she turned. "You know, there's no need...never mind. I'll be ready."

Ricardo let out a big breath, grateful they'd avoided another confrontation. He grabbed his phone, going to straight to speed dial. He'd promised her something special and he was damn sure going to deliver.

CHAPTER EIGHT

Ricardo shifted into fourth with gusto. With the top of his black Jeep off, the incredible summer day, and Julia sitting beside him in that tiny dress, memories of Texas couldn't compare with the here and now.

They drove north along Harbor Drive near downtown San Diego, the warm wind whipping against their faces, enjoying the sights like a couple of tourists. They had just passed the Coronado Bridge, its twinkling lights barely coming to life. Two Navy aircraft carriers were docked on the island, from what Ricardo could see. What he couldn't see but knew existed was an upscale, quaint, low-key community of Coronado. It looked peaceful from this distance.

Tethered sailboats of all sizes bobbed in the marina, their own tribute to the music provided by the soft waves. Their bare masts looked stark against the blue

skies. There was more than a sprinkling
of intriguing yachts and speedboats, and
their glossy finishes reflected the sun's
light. People jogged and skated along the
embarcadero, alone or in couples, with
dogs and without, looking perfectly
content.

Julia turned and smiled at him. He
was tempted to reach over and pull off
her Ray-Bans. He rather liked the look in
her eyes these days.

She leaned in close to him and shouted,
"Is it much farther?"

He looked ahead, the airport coming
into view, and changed lanes. San Diego,
he'd learned was true to historic loyalty.
The airport was known as Lindbergh
Field, not San Diego International
Airport. It was named after the famed
aviator because he'd commissioned Ryan
Airlines to build his "Spirit of St. Louis"
for the famed first nonstop flight from
New York to Paris. Lindbergh had
actually taken off from San Diego to New
York in the special plane.

Ricardo glanced over at Julia. Loyalty
was a rare commodity these days, but
maybe it abounded in San Diego and in
people like Julia. Damn but she made
him feel good. He hoped his surprise
would put a smile on her face and show

just how much her gumption meant to him.

Restaurant after restaurant lined the coastline, all the way up to Point Loma, he'd learned. He could see why she would think they were headed for one of them.

Again she asked, "Is it much farther?"

He shook his head and followed the off-ramp to a service and delivery route for the airport. It led them to an empty hangar. He pulled up to a reserved parking space and cut the engine.

"Should I wait here?" Julia lifted her glasses, and a look of uncertainty filled her eyes.

"No, ma'am. This is the end of the line." He lifted her overnight bag and his own duffle bag from the back of the Jeep. He opened her door and offered his hand to help her down.

She took his hand and squeezed it. "Montalvo, what are you doing?" she asked warily. "There's only a cafeteria inside this place. Please don't tell me that was your inspiration."

"Give me more credit than that, darlin'." He set the bags down and rubbed his shoulder without letting go of her hand.

"Are you okay? I can carry my own bag."

"Now you're really starting to hurt my feelings. It's just an old war wound, remember? From days on the football battlefield. Acts up every once in a while."

"And you, Montalvo, are sappy when you talk about the good old days. Can I take a raincheck on this outing?" She looked around as if she were looking for the quickest escape route.

He tucked her hand into the crook of his arm and picked up the bags. "Sorry. You have a one-way ticket and a promise that I won't bring up those old war stories tonight."

She pulled back like a kid being dragged to the dentist against her will. "Whoa. One-way ticket? I don't think so. I don't trust you."

"Smart woman." He laughed, holding her gaze. "How about just having a good time tonight and working on the trust issue later? I pegged you for having a sense of adventure."

She straightened abruptly, and the burnished-orange silky material of her dress eased around her body like flickering sparks and flames. "Sounds like a challenge to me, and you know I don't back away from a challenge. Lead on, Montalvo."

He took a good long, hard look at her and she stared right back. He could easily change his mind and take her to the safe parameters of her home and to the lonely ones of his. *She'll burn you, Montalvo.*

He shrugged. She'd pushed him to the point of no return with her comment about a challenge. He wasn't afraid of a little heat. "My kind of woman."

Walking through the hangar to the runway, Julia stopped in her tracks again. "Montalvo."

He didn't like that tone of voice. "Darlin'?"

"You can't be serious." She dropped his hand and walked slowly to the steps braced against his Longhorn Lear jet.

A man dressed as a pilot took the bags from Ricardo's hand. "Fifteen minutes, sir. Or when you're ready."

Ricardo touched her cheek and made her look at him. "Julia, honey. It's just a plane. It was gathering dust since I got here. The only way to get to the restaurant without taking a week off from work is flying this."

"This is yours?" Her voice cracked.

"One of them." His patience was wearing thin. He scraped his fingers through his hair. He only had the restaurant for the night. He could commiserate with Cinderella's midnight curfew. The details for the rest of the night depended on getting Julia's pretty ass onboard within the next five minutes.

"We have to get a move on. Jerry said we're ready to take off in fifteen minutes." He led her up the stairs. "Trust me, it looks better on the inside."

She seemed to come out of her trance. "I don't believe you." She managed a small, nervous laugh. "Do you always do things in such a big way? Sometimes you're such a Texas stereotype."

They stopped just outside the cockpit. "I don't think about big or small, darlin'. I think about what's right for the situation and then roll with that."

"Do you always roll into every town and roll over everything?"

"No." His jaw twitched. He had given her no reason to believe otherwise, but she wasn't going to lure him into that sticky area when all he wanted was to lure her far away from it, at least for tonight. He tilted back his hat so that she could see the truth in his eyes. "Do you always have to analyze people and judge their actions without knowing their intentions?"

A shocked look came over her face, and then she looked down at her feet. "No," she whispered.

"Then give me a break, at least tonight, darlin'. I have no hidden agenda. Just let me show you the restaurant and a good time. It's the least I can do. You've been working your ass off for me, when I know you'd rather have been anywhere else than in my office. I appreciate your graciousness more than you know."

She stared at him a moment more, seemed to struggle with a decision deep inside her. "Thank you for the invitation." She turned and walked into the seating area. "Show me that inspiration."

Ricardo raised his eyes and mouthed a silent *Thank you* before falling in behind her.

Graciousness? What's right for the situation? Julia would rather have been anywhere else than in the plush seat next to Ricardo, waiting for the next shocking words to come from his mouth. She was definitely out of her element around him and in the elegant jet, and he wasn't helping matters any by making her flustered.

"Buckle up, darlin'. We'll pour the champagne when we get the okay from Jerry."

She buckled up. She tried desperately to stay rigidly seated, but her body sank into the plush cushion until she wanted to curl her feet beneath her and ask for the champagne and a good book to go with it. She sighed.

Ricardo grinned. "That's more like it, darlin'."

The short parade of planes waiting for liftoff was a sight in itself from her vantage point. Ricardo had a flair for surprising her until she stood shell-shocked.

She glanced over at Ricardo, who seemed a thousand miles away already. He'd given her glimpses of himself with his generosity. Her heart saw his spirit, but her mind still saw the driven tycoon with no room for emotion in a business deal. She had crossed that line where he was concerned.

She looked back out the window, convinced that if she followed the rays of the setting sun, she'd be sure to find an answer to calm her turbulent heart. She was awed by the incredible splash of oranges and pinks in the sunset, perfection made even more so with Ricardo sitting next to her. That revelation scared her more than the thought of flying, even in a jet like this. *Business only,* she repeated to herself and tried to make herself believe it.

Truth was, she didn't want to talk about business at all.

"Champagne?" he asked, pulling her out of her reverie.

"Yes. That would be lovely." Julia drank a couple of glasses as the time passed, loosening her up to divulge more information about herself than was safe. When Ricardo answered a call on his cell phone, his deep voice lulled her to a dreamless sleep.

He shook her shoulder. "Hey, sleepyhead. We're here."

"Already?" She allowed herself a luxurious stretch until she saw Ricardo watching her with mischief in his eyes. She jerked down her arms. "Enjoying the show?"

"Enjoying you, darlin'."

"Is that so?" She allowed her gaze to slowly appreciate his body from head to boot. Instead of the nonchalant air she'd hoped for, a desire burned right through her, throwing her off balance. "Well. You shouldn't. That's not polite."

His bold laugh cut the tension. "Just looking. Have I been out of line with you?"

"No. A perfect gentleman, much to my surprise."

"I appreciate the finer things in life, and you are, by far, one of those finer things. Today at least. Excuse me."

She watched him in stunned silence.
Too bold and breathtaking for his own
good. Or hers. She didn't trust herself to
speak.

He rose and pulled their bags out from
behind their seats. "Hope you got enough
rest. That's all you get until tomorrow."
He looked at her with feigned innocence.
"Would you like to freshen up?"

She peered out the small porthole.
"Where are we?"

"New York."

"New York? You've got to be kidding!"
She hopped on her seat and peered out
the window again, the darkness and
twinkling lights revealing nothing. "This
is unbelievable. I've actually been
kidnapped."

"I prefer to think of it as whisking you
away." He put down the bags and walked
over to her. Taking her hand, he said, "I
just want do something nice for you. You
work hard, you're worried about your
grandfather and aunt, and the smile that
should grace your face isn't there enough.
I thought a change of pace would do us
both good. I hope you can let loose and
enjoy yourself."

She took a deep breath to steady her
pounding heart. When was the last time
someone had given a damn about her

happiness? When had she? "I'd really like that," she said and meant it.

"Then get a move on. You missed the best sights when we were flying in. Now you'll have to see them from the car."

"Give me five, then." Adrenaline rushed through her. Was it because of the unknown surprises still up Ricardo's sleeve, or the prospect of spending a night alone with him, away from work and family? She wouldn't dwell on it. She was determined to have a good time.

Refreshed, she walked out of the luxurious bathroom. Decorated in teakwood and brass, the accessories were top of the line, just like the other wonderful perks she'd seen throughout the plane. She glanced at the door at the back of the plane, wondering what could possibly be behind it.

He hustled her out of the plane and into a limo, as if he were racing against the clock. "Does the New York pace automatically do this to you or are you late for something?"

"Don't ask." He laughed and sank back into his seat, draping an arm casually across her shoulders.

They drove around Manhattan for nearly two hours, Ricardo pointing out the sights like a tour guide with his own twist on everything from the United

Nations world sculpture in front of the building to the eighty-seventh floor at the Empire State Building.

"Times Square! Being here on New Year's Eve has been on my bucket list forever." Julia forgot about being careful, her joy at being near Broadway with its rows of theaters too much for her to sustain any kind of cool façade.

"We can make that happen."

"Ricardo. This is too much already. It's perfect. Thank you. I've always dreamed of seeing Broadway. Now I know I'll come back."

"I'd love to bring you back if you'd let me. No business, then, I promise."

Her heart sank. She didn't want to think about business. She didn't want Ricardo to be the adversary anymore. She didn't want to fight for property Ricardo should have known could never be for sale.

"Look, darlin'." Ricardo lowered his voice and waited until she looked at him. "I hate bringing it up, but that's why we came in the first place. If you see the restaurant, maybe you'll see more clearly where I'm coming from. I want to lay it all out on the table for you, sort of strip myself down to bare bones, if you will, and answer any questions you have, but I don't want to talk business all night long."

Her mouth went unexpectedly dry. Talk about double entendre. Their business proposals were not what she saw lying naked on the table. Stripping him down had potential.

Perhaps it would be safer to keep it on a business level as long as possible. "Business talk is fine. I need to get my work for you done so that I can move on and you can back off. It's going to take a lot more than some special restaurant to convince me that what you're doing to my family is the only solution to your parking problem. I'm trying to leave the emotional part out of this, as per your instructions, but I don't even see your logic."

He took his hat off and slapped it on his knee. "Give me a break, Julia. Leave the emotion out of it? You did the exact opposite." He pulled his arm off her shoulders and clasped his hands between his legs. "Damn it—you make me feel everything I shouldn't in a business deal. Does that make you feel any better?"

She shrugged. "A little." *A lot,* she thought. *This is a step in the right direction.* She let out a breath of relief.

"I think we're both strung out on this one." He banged on the sliding window between them and the driver. "Texas, please."

The limo pulled up to the corner of Broadway and Forty-Eighth. Ricardo put his hat back on. He held the car door open for her and offered his arm as they strolled silently up the street. She was amazed at his chameleon ability. He looked just as much at ease here as he had in San Diego, as he did in the plane, with his boots on or with a thousand-dollar suit defining his muscular body. She turned away before she could think any other thoughts about his body.

Julia took a deep breath, taking in the lights and marquees, huge neon billboards and unique advertising displays. From her readings, she knew thousands and thousands of storefronts, restaurants, and hotels were crammed into one square mile along this area. Electricity charged the air as people bustled about with an energy that swept them along at an incredible pace.

One of the most powerful and influential places in the world, Manhattan had to be an advertising executive's dream come true. Still, she imagined the cutthroat competitiveness could take its toll in a hurry. She liked the idea that some of her clients were based in New York and were perfectly content with her work. She was perfectly content working out of San Diego, a sleepy little town compared to New York. It was nice for a visit, though, for a shot of adrenaline and a touch of magic and electricity.

She ventured a glance at Ricardo's profile and sucked in her breath. His rugged good looks and confident air charged her with an undeniably electric response to *him*. It unnerved her, knowing how many times in the past few months she'd had to will her heart to steady itself when he walked into the studio or stood next to her, looking over her work.

Knowing he did that to her in a safe environment, she suddenly realized it may have been a big mistake coming here.

Here, alone with him and no work to keep her hands busy, she could picture her hands wandering the broad ridges of his chest in slow, easy movements, appreciating the strength and hardness there. In his arms on the dance floor back home, he'd held her as if she were more precious than a handful of gems. That feeling overwhelmed her at times.

She wanted those arms to enfold her and let them forget the nasty business lying between them like some Godforsaken chasm. She wanted to find answers to the questions that plagued them more each day.

They reached the restaurant just in the nick of time. *Texas, Texas Restaurant and Saloon,* the sign read. Next to it was another sign. *Closed. Private Party.*

He reached for the doorknob.

"Did you read that?"

"Who do you think they're referring to?" He pulled the door open and then clicked it locked behind them.

"You rented out the entire restaurant? On a Friday night? In Manhattan?" She enunciated each few words with disbelief.

"Just until midnight." He tucked her hand in the crook of his arm, practically dragging her along. "Cinderella time. Come on. We don't have much time and I want you to see everything. I love this place."

The place was incredible. The decorations were an eclectic mix of contemporary and traditional, each object colorfully telling its own version of Texas history and where the great state stood now.

"Take a look around, darlin'. Do you see where the idea for a themed restaurant of this magnitude came to me?"

"I'd say." Over the longest bar Julia had ever seen hung the stereotypical longhorns. Rows of bottles, at least ten deep, were interrupted by a small sign that boldly stated *Lone Star Beer, Best in Texas*. Sitting right in the middle of the bar was an angry-looking, stuffed armadillo. Glasses shaped like boots were crammed into a corner of the bartender's work area.

A huge chandelier hung from an incredibly high ceiling, its soft lights casting confetti shadows onto the floor and walls. There was one red-brick wall with a fireplace in the corner. Prints by different artists of the battle at the Alamo decorated the walls, along with maps of Texas in varying sizes.

Two oversized bronze fans whirled lazily, keeping step to the soulful, vintage wails belted out by Patsy Cline and Loretta Lynn to the dreamy voices of Tim McGraw and Luke Bryan that had filled the air since they walked into the restaurant.

Ricardo, on the other hand, was hearing his own beat, Julia thought. His excitement was contagious as he jumped from place to place, showing her everything like a kid with a favorite music app to share.

"Your offer to work for me was the best thing that could ever have happened to me, darlin'." He raised her hands to his lips and kissed them. "You've brought back an excitement with your work that I haven't felt since the first time I walked in here and saw all the possibilities. I wish the circumstances surrounding the project were different."

She shrugged, but for all the nonchalance, she couldn't quite quell the anxiety in the pit of her stomach. She had to convince him through her work that he—and the studio—would be better off side by side. "I know you have the resources and you could have shut us down in a blink, but you've been a gentleman by sticking to your word and giving me time. That means a lot to me. You won't be sorry. I'm confident we'll find that middle ground."

"Keep talkin', darlin'. At this very moment, there's nothing I want more than an alternative."

He had a way of surprising her right out of the blue, rendering her speechless. A rarity. She seemed to always be on the defensive around him, ready to put up her dukes and punch him back across any line he dared cross before she was ready, but his surprises were a welcome relief.

"How about a boot drink to forget about work for a little while?"

"Sounds dangerous."

"Depends on how many. Since we're not driving, drink away."

He led her to a table with a white tablecloth, candlelight, and sparkling silverware. The other tables were casual, miniature picnic tables. A placard on the table showed a glass shaped like a boot. The list of ingredients in the various boot drinks seemed endless.

"May I recommend the San Antonio Rose for you? It has tequila, rum, and a few fruit juices and liqueurs thrown in for good measure. Very appropriate. A rose for a rose."

"You expect me to drink that and walk out of here?"

A wicked gleam lit his eyes. "I can always carry you out. It would be my pleasure."

It would be like crossing to the dark side. The point of no return if she gave in to her desires and his attempts to make her forget work. "I'm sure it would."

He partially stood to reach in the seat behind him and pulled out a beautiful, perfect yellow rose. "Speaking of roses— this is for you."

Her heart fluttered in that way she was getting used to around him. "When you're nice, you're too nice, Ricardo." She reached across the table and covered his hand with her own. "Stop being so nice."

The surprise that flashed across his face eased back into a calm façade. "Never."

His thumb brushed against the top of her hand, hypnotically stroking the tension from her mind and body. Replacing it was a slow, warming heat fanning through her at an alarming rate. She bit her bottom lip and waited.

Ricardo cleared his throat. "Dance with me. I'll show you a slow two-step."

She started to pull her hand away. "I don't know how."

"Please. You're the dancer and a quick study. Let me show you." He stood and bowed, holding his hand out to her. Linda Ronstadt crooned a haunting rendition of "Desperado."

Julia took Ricardo's outstretched hand. "This music is so slow and heart-wrenching. How can you dance to it?"

He pulled her tight against him, the movement of his hips slow and deliberate, unbearably sexy, and Julia's body responded. "There's something to be said for slow." He dipped downward. She gasped at the feel of his leg between hers, a flaming desire instantly filling her.

His voice turned husky. "This song isn't heart-wrenching if you're with the right person, Julia. Listen."

Ricardo sang low, never missing a beat. He was serenading her through voice and body. He pulled their clasped hands to the now-familiar position against his chest. She turned their hands so that he could also feel her heartbeat.

Julia closed her eyes and leaned into him, surrendered herself to him, their feet gliding smoothly. She smelled him, a musky mix of Armani Code and the incomparable scent of Ricardo himself. She felt his rough palm against hers, the pressure of his large hand on the small of her back sending shivers skittering over her arms, and heard him singing for her, and her alone.

They moved slowly, creating their own small dance floor, not needing much space for their barely moving bodies. His song floated over her, whispers and promises cradling hopes and desires. Her fears slowly dissipated with the ending strains of the sad guitar.

"You better let somebody love you, before it's too late." Ricardo ended the song in perfect harmony to Linda's haunting voice. He pulled away from Julia for a moment, looking into her eyes with desire she knew only mirrored her own. Their feet stopped moving.

With no musical accompaniment, he sang the line again, nuzzling his lips against her hair. "You better let somebody love you, before it's too late."

Her tears came from nowhere. She slipped her hand from his shoulder and slipped it around his neck, holding on for dear life. She pressed her body against his, wanting him more than seemed sane.

He'd tore into her family. He'd threatened everything she stood for and believed in. He'd shaken her to her very core. Against every rational thought, she'd gone and fallen in love with him.

"Shh. I didn't thinking my singing was that bad, darlin'." His voice cracked as he wiped a tear from her cheek. "We were supposed to be celebrating, remember?"

"This wasn't supposed to happen, Ricardo." His arms enveloped her. He let her cry, let her cling to him, let her dream. When she had quieted, he brushed back her hair from her face and kissed her tenderly.

"Some teacher I am. Do you want to try and follow my lead again?" His hands slipped from her waist and he ran them slowly down her backside.

She shook her head. Enough. This was torture. "Why don't you follow mine?" She rose on her toes and cupped his face in her hands. She kissed him long and slow, and the breath that had quieted refused to stay quiet any longer.

He pulled away, seeming confused and a little wary of losing control over the situation. "Are you hungry? They're ready to feed us."

"I'm not hungry for food." She held his gaze. "Just want to taste you."

Without a word he nodded, reached in his pocket with a somewhat shaky hand, and threw a large wad of bills onto the table. He lifted her into his arms easily. Carrying her to the door, he broke their kiss only long enough to whisper, "I'll feed you later."

She hoped it was much, much later.

She couldn't still the throbbing of her lips. Their kisses in the limo to the airport had grown more passionate with every passing minute. Their hands had touched and caressed, lingered and stroked each other until it was maddening. And yet, they'd refrained. They'd both felt an urgency to get home, perhaps to make things right, to make sure they could work things out.

"I'll bring you back to New York some other time," he'd said. "I promise."

And Julia had believed him.

Julia held Ricardo's hand easily, as if they'd been doing this all their lives. She looked out the Learjet's window, amazed at the smooth ride, the quiet engines, and that she was there at all.

The voice in her head told her repeatedly that she was making a big mistake. She didn't want to listen to it. Home was too far away and Ricardo was too close for comfort. "Can I get up yet?"

"Sure," Ricardo said. "It's safe now."

She paced up and down the aisle, each time coming closer to the closed door at the end. She wanted him. Wanted him in there. Wanted him against her. In her. She turned to head back down aisle again, more than ready to take the lead and and take care of business if he wouldn't.

Ricardo blocked her way. "What's going on? You're acting like a firecracker in a barrel."

She tried to get around him. "Just my second wind kicking in, I guess. I didn't hear you."

"You wouldn't hear fireworks if they went off beside you." He pulled her close. "I can think of a better way to diffuse that energy or light up those fireworks— whichever you prefer."

"You are *so* subtle. Would you start like this?" She ran her wayward hands up his incredible chest, over his shoulders and around his back, sliding down to his backside and lingering there.

He moaned and that undid her.

All her doubts about the two of them disappeared. Surprised at her boldness, she waited, her breath coming out in shallow spurts, his heat seeping through her pores.

"Darlin', I, I..."

"You? Speechless?" She caressed his backside, enjoying the circular motion of her hands and the look on his face.

"Sometimes words are overrated. There are other ways to say things." He opened the door behind her, whisked her through, and shut it behind them.

Her eyes grew wide. "A bed?"

"We'll get there. Don't rush it."

"That's not what I meant."

"Then what did you mean?"

He didn't let her answer, covering her mouth with his. He backed her against the door, pressing his body against hers.

He hiked up her dress a bit and slowly ran his warm hands up and down her bare thighs, coming perilously close to her panties each time. He pulled his hands away.

Julia moaned. "No fair. Absolutely no fair."

"You started it." He held her by the waist, let his hands travel her torso, his thumbs brushing the sides of her breasts, driving her crazy.

She took his hand to stop its wandering and placed it gently on top of her breast.

"My, my, Julia. You are *so* subtle."

"There's a time and a place for everything. Subtlety included." Her fingertips grazed his hand and followed down the muscular forearm and back up to his shoulder. She pressed against him, trapping his hand until it had nowhere else to go. "And don't you know when to take a hint?" she whispered.

"You bet, darlin'." His hand firmly squeezed her breast, his thumb brushing her nipple. He pushed her back gently until they were up against the door. He leaned down and took her breast in his mouth, the silky material a poor, ragged armor against the exquisite torture.

His mouth traveled up her neck, touched her earlobe, and found her lips. "Let me make you happy, Julia."

Her response was lost in their kiss. Their lips parted, allowing them to deepen their kiss, finding a rhythm to match their swaying hips.

He pressed against her. Her hips rocked slowly, making their own hypnotic music. His hands roamed harder, more deliberately, not missing an inch of her body. He finally slipped them under her dress, under that last protective shield, and jerked her toward him. His fingers found her, slipped into her, released her.

"Damn!" She wrapped her arms around him. Her breathing quickened. One magical stroke and she sucked in her breath. His knowing fingers—relentless, tireless, fearless—brought her to the brink until her body tightened, tightened, tightened around them. She closed her eyes and tried to still her shaking limbs. Her release came slow and complete, her body warm and pulsing.

She tilted back her head and covered her eyes with her hand. "Oh, honey. I've never, ever..." Her mind went blank.

"Julia speechless? My, my." Ricardo chuckled. "Darlin', let me try something else to keep you quiet a little longer."

"It won't work." She punched his chest, tried to squirm out of his embrace.

"That's a challenge if I ever heard one." He ran his hand down her body, from her neck to her stomach, and stopped. She didn't want him to stop.

Her resolve didn't last long. Ricardo kissed her neck, his lips hot and moist, instantly flaming her desire.

Her hands hurriedly unbuttoned his shirt, and she restrained herself from ripping it off him. She struggled with his belt buckle and gave up. She stroked him, dying to touch him, to feel him inside her. "Damn it, Ricardo, is that your own version of a chastity belt? You have too many clothes on. Help me."

He laughed and pressed against her. "Your wish is my command." He tore off his shirt and threw it at their feet.

Pressing herself against the door, she watched him in awe. In less than a minute, his glorious body was naked and ready for her. He hoisted her up, his hands firmly holding her backside, kissing her, crooning to her, loving her like she'd never known.

She wrapped her legs and arms around his body, more than ready for him.

He carried her to the bed and set her down there gently. "Now *you* have too many clothes on." He lifted the dress over her head, pulled off her panties, and let his gaze roam, drinking her in, inch by inch.

She swallowed hard. He ran his finger down her cheek and across her throbbing lips. He kissed her tenderly, then rested his forehead against hers. "Heaven help me, Julia."

She pulled away, needing to see him. Despair looked out from his eyes, echoing her own. She reached for his hands. The magic in their touch had made her forget everything except the here and now.

And that he'd taken her body and heart in one fell swoop.

What if they only had tonight? She lay back and pulled him next to her. Their longing seeped through their fingertips until their bodies heated to unbearable proportions.

She was ready for him, would always be ready for him. And yet, reality hit. "Do you have protection, Ricardo?"

He stopped his wandering hands and looked at her, an amused glint lighting his eyes. "I was hoping you'd ask."

A warning tone escaped her lips. "Ricardo."

He couldn't be as innocent as he tried to look. He hopped up from the bed and walked over to a small closet. He pulled down a box, carried it to her on the palm of his hand and set it in front of her.

She looked at him warily, then pulled back the two flaps. She couldn't help but laugh. "That's a lot of condoms. Thinking big again, Ricardo?"

He shoved the box off the bed and slid in next to her, planting a big kiss on her open mouth. "No, darlin', just *hoping* big, where you're concerned."

He reached down and picked up one of the condoms that had fallen out of the box. "Let me help you with that," she whispered. As her hands wrapped around him, then lingered, then stroked, his sharp intake made her look up. "You ok?"

"Give me a second."

It looked like he was counting to ten. "I won't last very long if you keep doing that." He reached for her hair that had fallen over him as she leaned in close.

"It's a long flight. We can try again."

He laughed in that wonderful way of his, giving her a chance to see his six pack ripple. And the way the image and sound rained over her, making her tingle, making her not want to wait one more minute.

"Slow down. Just for a minute." He slipped out from underneath her and pushed her gently against the pillows. "Give me just a second." He nuzzled her neck and his warm breath stirred such longing, she pulled him tight against her. She closed her eyes and disappeared into the magic of his kisses, on her cheeks, her eyelids, the tip of her nose until they reached her lips. And the electricity scorched her.

He pulled away as if he felt the sting of it too. "Julia, I never meant to hurt you. That's not what I want." He kissed her again. "I'm not a bad guy."

Was he trying to convince her or himself? "I know," she said simply, and believed it.

As he slid inside her, she faced what she'd known for a long time. He wasn't a bad guy. He was the kind of guy who moved her and made her see how well they fit together when they weren't on opposite sides of the business fence.

She looked into his eyes, feeling every slow seductive motion of his body against hers, and wrapped her arms around his neck, drawing him closer for another kiss. She didn't want him to forget her once he left for Texas.

For now, she kissed him deeply. She couldn't let him go. Wouldn't let him go. Every inhalation was him. Every moan was for him. Every delicious feel was from him. He tasted wicked and sensual. And tender and vulnerable. And for this moment she was lost to him. As their kisses grew deeper, she couldn't get him close enough until she twined her legs around him. Finally, finally, they were lifted to the heavens, leaving reality far behind.

They didn't touch ground again until the jet landed back home.

CHAPTER NINE

Ricardo kicked the metal trash can across the front office. It hit the wall with a resounding thud, its contents scattering to the floor like confetti. He stomped over to it, ready to send it flying again. Instead, he stood over it, breathing heavily. His eyes lit on Julia's discarded work. He picked up one crumpled paper and saw the drawing of his restaurant, surrounded not by asphalt, but by grass. A bridge joined it to her aunt's studio.

Damn it. He crumpled it up again and dropped it near his feet.

She hadn't answered her phone, hadn't opened her door to his incessant pounding in the two days since they'd returned from New York. She had shown up at dance lessons but with new students in tow—a young couple and their three children. She'd given him nothing more than a cursory nod and pawned him off on Elvira. He tried to follow her out of the studio after the lessons but was surrounded by the clan, talking to him excitedly about Family Night. By the time he'd made it outside, she was long gone.

He leaned against the wall of his office and slid down until his butt hit the floor. He never let emotions get in the way of business. But then he had never intended to fall in love with Julia.

The realization flowed over him. He thought that having concrete poured over him inch by inch, crushing his chest until he couldn't breathe, would give him the same feeling.

Bad timing. Bad situation. Bad business. He banged his head against the wall and his Stetson popped off and flew forward, landing at his feet. The woman had put some spell on him. Here he was repeating everything three times, as if that could help clarify his position or make sense out of anything that involved Julia.

It was a matter of principle. He didn't need another restaurant to make sure his family was taken care of beyond any doubt. Logic screamed that he'd taken every precaution so that his family was now set up for life, and he, himself, wouldn't be in his father's shoes and lose his entire life savings, job, home, and everything that mattered in one fell swoop.

All that mattered was Julia. His chances for convincing her to give him a chance beyond the boardroom were slim to none if she kept avoiding him. He spread out the drawing between his feet and tried to smooth out the wrinkles. Squinting against the waning light didn't affect his opinion of her work. It was beautiful, unique, and most certainly plausible.

A knock sounded on the door. "Go away!" He wasn't in the mood for any company.

"Rick, it's Chase!"

"Then you'd really better go away. I won't be held responsible for any physical damage."

Chase poked his head through the doorway. "I'm a big boy. And I can easily handle you, even on my worst day." He flipped on the light switch next to the door before letting himself in.

Ricardo glared at him, only too aware of what he had to see: Ricardo on the floor, the trash can lying on its side, the strewn papers around him. Entrepreneurship at its best.

Chase set down a huge O's Restaurant bag stuffed with smaller bags of what had to be breadsticks, the best in town. The heavy aroma of garlic wafted through the air and Rick's stomach growled. Chase walked past him, into his office, and came out carrying the oversized ice chest filled with sodas. "Do you want to talk about it?"

He put the ice chest down near Ricardo's feet and sat on it. It creaked in protest, like the stirrings of an avalanche.

Ricardo shook his head. "No." He squeezed his clasped hands tighter.

"Is it Julia?"

Just the mention of her name made his blood boil again. He couldn't control the way he turned to mush when she was near him. "What makes you think that?" He grabbed a handful of papers from the floor and stuffed them into the trash can.

"Lucky guess?" Chase shrugged when Ricardo didn't return his smile. He picked up the paper between Ricardo's feet. "Julia's work. It's great. Could be the answer you've been looking for."

"She played me."

"No. Julia wouldn't do that."

"I took her to New York and things happened that had nothing to do with business, the restaurant, her aunt's livelihood."

Chase remained annoyingly silent—for a moment. "And that's a problem because…?"

"Because now she's ignoring me. Like none of it ever happened. Like it's business as usual. Maybe she just used me to make me soft and give in."

"No one uses you, Rick. Even if you're hot for her, you wouldn't let her use you. Not for business anyway. Maybe she's just scared you all crossed the line. Which means more is on the line with your businesses."

Scared? "It was mutual."

"It? If you're talking about sex, get over that. I think Julia's fallen for you and doesn't like it or know what to do about it."

"She's driving me crazy."

"You're scared. That woman's gotten under your skin." He walked over to Ricardo and tapped him hard on the chest. "And she got in here. Why are you fighting it?"

Chase was right. He'd gone soft, letting a woman dictate the direction of his business. "It's business. No emotion." His voice sounded foreign to him. Almost ridiculous.

"That's all you've talked about, Rick. Keeping emotion out of this deal. You're not doing a very good job of it today."

Ricardo leaned his head back against the wall. "I know what the fuck I've said. She's changed the game plan for me. I was ready to leave here, to leave the studio intact but if she wants nothing to do with me, then why should I put my family at risk?"

"You've set your family up for this lifetime and the next, Rick. Give it a break. Give yourself a break. Give her a break. She did her job and offered alternatives that are completely viable."

Ricardo stood, his heart heavy. "I can't. We'll go through with the original plans. I just got sidetracked by Julia, but we need the parking lot."

"No we don't. I won't be a part of it."

"You're taking their side?"

"There doesn't have to be a side Rick. Look at what Julia's proposing. It's the best alternative and both businesses can thrive on it. I feel it."

Why wouldn't she talk to him? What had happened in the last two days to make her change her mind about him? What had he done wrong? He leaned on the desk. Maybe he should just cut his losses and leave San Diego before he could do any more damage—or she cut him off at the knees. "I'll think about it."

"Not everything's set in stone. Compromise is not weakness." Chase slapped his hands on his thighs and stood. "Enough of that. We'd better get a move on."

Ricardo stared at the twitching muscle in Chase's jawline, at the grim line of his lips, at the rigid posture. Definitely an avalanche ready to take everything with it. "Where are we going?" he growled.

"Family Night at the dance studio."

"Can't do it."

"Oh, yes, you can, and you will. We already told them we'd be there. Short of killing you on the spot, there's no excuse for not going. You need to suck it up, walk across the street and let them see what kind of man you really are." He shrugged. "They already like you, you know."

Ricardo knew that. But did Julia? "Give me a couple of minutes."

"Sure. Can I wear your hat tonight?"

"Not that one." He looked at what used to be a pristine white Stetson, now graying. Upon close inspection, he saw that the rim was frayed and fingerprints indented the front, where he always touched and tipped it. "There's an extra one in the closet."

He shut the bathroom door behind him and filled a large plastic tumbler with running water. He leaned over the deep sink and emptied the cup over his head. It was a poor substitute, but it would have to do. He needed an ice-cold lake to jump into, to shake his head clear of unwanted thoughts of Julia and tame his body back into submission.

He let the water drip off the tips of his hair and onto his face. He stared at the sorry image in the mirror, then yanked the towel off the rack and rubbed it hard over his face. He'd steer clear of Julia tonight, but that brought another unnerving thought to mind. Lorenza would nab him and badger him for details. Maybe Chase would feel it his duty to jump in front of that speeding train to save him. Or maybe he'd be delighted to throw Ricardo to the wolves, after the way he'd been acting lately.

Rolling up the sleeves of his denim shirt, he walked out to join Chase. "Thanks for the kick in the butt. I needed it."

"Yeah, you did. Pity party's over. Ready to go?"

"Yes. Wait a minute." He walked over to his desk and studied Julia's drawing as objectively as he could. "How feasible would it be to use something like this versus what we have?"

Chase studied the drawing. "It really beats putting in the parking lot, Rick. The changes Julia shows here wouldn't even affect the structure. They'd be more in line with the flow of Old Town, enhancing it as a historic landmark. She certainly knows the area, the potential here, and she has a keen eye for working *with* the design, not against it."

Ricardo strummed his fingers on the desktop. It looked too promising, just like she herself had a few nights ago. "I don't know. I need the parking lot. It's a guarantee to draw in clientele because you know prime parking spots are scarce in Old Town."

Chase smoothed a hand over the paper, ignoring him, it seemed. "Cobblestone walkways are a nice touch, bringing people from any point in Old Town right to the restaurant's front door. If you implement valet parking, this is the answer that can satisfy everyone."

Ricardo could easily offer primo valet service and haul those cars a couple of miles if he had to. That wasn't the real issue. There were alternatives. It wouldn't be like he was giving in or showing emotion as a sign of weakness in any way if he accepted Julia's ideas.

As a matter of fact, in ideal times, his dance club could work in conjunction with the studio and offer those who'd taken lessons half-price for a cover charge. He could sponsor dance contests or send potential students to Elvira. He could sweep Julia off her feet like he had once before.

A look of concern crossed Chase's face. "Julia invested too much emotion into this project, and you're not investing enough. There has to be a middle ground between the two of you."

The middle ground was quicksand, as far as Rick was concerned. Hell, anything around the general vicinity where Julia stood would suck him under. He was far from ready for anything of that magnitude.

"This *is* the middle ground." She saw their night together as a mistake. The one time he'd opened up to her had backfired. She had weakened him. No more.

He set his jaw. "She's driving me crazy and I'm not thinking clearly. I'm not budging, Chase. A parking lot is something tangible I can count on, and I know it will enhance my business. Anything else is a crapshoot."

That included his chances with Julia. He'd made a mistake assuming anything, and it wouldn't happen again.

He swept Julia's plans onto the floor. "We'll proceed with the original plans and then I'll head on back to Texas."

Chase calmly picked the plans off the floor and put them back on the desk. "Back to that again? Back to Texas? You can't run away from Julia."

"I'm not running—from her or anyone. I've spent far too much time and effort in San Diego. It's time to plan the next set of restaurants."

That would keep him more than occupied. San Diego would fade into one of its glorious sunsets and he could pick himself up by the bootstraps and kick some more butt, far away from here.

"What about the restaurant? And my job?"

"All yours. The restaurant stays, I go."

"What about Julia?"

"She'll be fine." He couldn't say the same about himself.

"It's not always that black and white. Why don't you think..."

A rap sounded on the front door. "Ricardo? Chase?"

Old Spice aftershave announced Don Carlos's presence even before he stepped into the room. "Boys, I was getting worried about you. Everyone's waiting."

"Sorry, Don Carlos. I was waylaid."

"Ah, what did Julia do now?" He wagged a bony finger at them and smiled. "The neighbors told me you two came in awfully late the other night. You're going to start those tongues wagging again."

He shook his head. "Never mind. Tell me when we have an hour to kill. Lorenza's already lined up dances with both of you. Too bad we're not raising money for some worthy cause and charging for each dance."

Ricardo looked at Chase and he knew he was thinking the same thought. "Not on Family Night, Don Carlos, but that's a great idea. We'll do the fundraiser some other night—pull out all the bells and whistles and advertise heavily, really draw in the crowds."

"I'll hold you to that. Until then, we better get a move on." Don Carlos reached down to take one handle of the ice chest. He abruptly brought his palm to the middle of his chest and staggered away from them.

"Don Carlos!" Ricardo raced over to him, threw his arm around his waist, and lifted the weak old man into the nearby chair.

"Leave me, boy! I'm fine," Don Carlos wheezed. He snapped, "You and Julia are the same. It's just my indigestion flaring up, damn it, and you treat me like I'm an invalid."

"I didn't mean any disrespect." He knelt by the old man who had become his friend and recognized in him the same stubbornness of his own father.

A fierce sense of protectiveness filled him. It did nothing to get rid of the acrid taste of foreboding in his mouth. It had to be worse for Don Carlos. "Chase, get some water. Don Carlos, just sit tight for a few minutes. Then we'll go."

"We're already late." He struggled to sit up straighter. His eyes watered with the effort.

"Then we'll make a grand entrance." He took the glass of water from Chase and raised it to Don Carlos's trembling lips.

He took a small sip and sat back. His hand finally dropped from his chest into his lap.

"Feeling better?" Ricardo wanted a resounding yes for an answer, but Don Carlos looked paler than his fair skin should be.

"I'm fine, son. Just don't treat me..."

"I know, I know. Like an invalid. You are one stubborn old man."

"It takes one to know one."

Ricardo chuckled. "Hey, what did I ever do to you?"

He gently took off Don Carlos's glasses and laid them on the floor next to him. Thankfully, he didn't resist. Ricardo dipped his fingers in the unused water, shook them off, and ran them over Don Carlos's flushed cheeks. From the corner of his eye he saw Chase looking mighty uncomfortable.

"Not to me, son." Don Carlos closed his eyes. "It's you and Julia. You remind me of me and my wife. Julia gets that feistiness from her." He smiled. Color came back into his cheeks.

He sat up straight and opened his eyes. The worst had passed. His face softened into countless creases. He patted Ricardo's shoulder. "You're a good boy and you'll do what is right. But don't lose sight of what's important. You don't want to be alone and have no one to share all your success. What good is that? Help me up."

He slid to the edge of his seat and grasped Ricardo's arm. "We've kept the women waiting for us and that's not right." He pulled Ricardo's shoulder down so he could whisper in his ear. "I even brought in a friend of Julia's for Chase. That boy will have fun tonight."

Ricardo was relieved to find Don Carlos's grip as strong and sure as his words. "Don Carlos, later tonight Chase and I want to announce a new plan that will leave the studio intact. It should set everyone's minds at ease."

His bright blue eyes bore into Ricardo. "Thank you, son. Now I can rest easy." He pointed to his glasses and Ricardo bent to pick them up.

Don Carlos started walking, his step slow, followed by Ricardo and Chase. Ricardo offered his arm and was surprised when he took it. He wished he could hoist Don Carlos up and carry him across the street. He didn't want to see him struggle.

Ricardo glanced at the upper level of Elvira's dance studio, her living quarters. His throat constricted.

Julia stood on the tiny balcony. An incredible sunset slashed across the sky in muted oranges, pinks, and soft blues around her. The colors crowned her, seemed to stem from her, competed with her own vibrancy.

She leaned on the flower boxes, the bright pink and purple flowers and wispy overhanging vines picking up the regal, deep purple of her sleeveless dress. Ricardo wanted to kneel before her like some knight from long-ago times to pledge his allegiance to her and her family.

Ricardo tripped, bringing Don Carlos to a complete stop. He clasped his other hand over Don Carlos's hand, to keep the grip firm.

"What is it now, boy?" he asked impatiently.

Like a fool, Ricardo couldn't answer. He caught Julia's gaze and held it.

She smiled at him and waved. "Ricardo! Grandpa! Chase!"

Don Carlos slowly looked up.

She looked back and forth between Ricardo and her grandfather, and her smile faltered. Without another word, she turned and ran from the balcony.

Julia dashed down the stairs. The buzz of activity already filled the festively decorated studio. She pulled away from arms that tried to stop her, from the voices that called her name.

She made it to the front door just as Ricardo, Grandpa, and Chase reached it. "Ricardo?"

"He said it was indigestion."

"And you believed him?"

"No, darlin', I didn't."

There was an unflinching look in his eyes, a quiet sort of desperation she knew connected them. She nodded, took her grandpa's hand, and slipped it into the crook of her arm.

"Mija, you talk about me like I'm not even here," he said, his voice not angry, just tired. He pulled his hand free. "I love you." He kissed her cheek and turned to face Ricardo. "And even you, son, but I'm feeling better now, and my dance card is full. You two can follow my lead."

He strutted off, the spring back in his step. He was clearly in his element. Approaching a cluster of women, he bowed and said something Julia couldn't hear, making them giggle like schoolgirls.

"Stubborn old man," she said, shaking her head.

"I told him as much." Ricardo shoved his hands into his pants pockets.

Ricardo smelled divine and looked even better. "You told him?" she asked. "How'd he react?"

"He said it takes one to know one."

Julia laughed. "Sounds like something he would say." She glanced over at Grandpa in the midst of the admiring women. "I'll have to watch him carefully tonight."

"We can take shifts." Ricardo's gaze was on him, too, and Julia's breath caught at the serious look on his face. There was no mistaking the concern in the drawn eyebrows or the set line of his lips.

"Thank you," she croaked. She licked her own lips, achingly aware that his mouth had kissed her for hours, so many hours that she'd risen light-headed and had all but swooned on their flight back to San Diego. His lips had roamed every inch of her traitorous body, making her feel heaven on earth, his kisses lifting her far from this world. She touched her fingertips to her lips, still able to feel him there, taste him, desire him as she'd never desired anyone.

"You've been ignoring me." Ricardo shifted his gaze to her, and it slowly traveled the length of her body.

She crossed her arms over her chest, her nipples responding to his long, lazy look. They tingled against the soft velvet of her dress. She ached for him to touch her again, to make her breasts and every part of her body respond to the most exquisite, excruciating joy she'd ever known. "I don't want to. I have to."

He held her gaze steady. "Why, darlin'?"

"Because I'm not dragging my heart into the middle of this mess. You were right. There can't be any emotion in a business transaction." Staying away from him since New York had been pure agony.

"What kind of guy do you think I am?" His eyes blazed. "I've been wracking my brain to find that alternative we were talking about because I want this business over with, nothing between us, a clean slate. We can make your plans work. We'll make them work."

The chill that invaded her body made her wish for a sweater, knowing full well it wasn't a sweater she needed, much less wanted. He looked at her through undeniably long lashes and the penetrating gaze that would make her feel naked even if she were decked out in full-fledged diving gear.

"Ricardo, you scare the hell out of me professionally, but even more so, personally. And I don't know what to do about it."

Lorenza stood with her circle of friends on the opposite side of the room, blatantly pointing toward Julia and Ricardo. *Where's a rock to hide under when you need one?* Julia thought.

"Let's talk later. We have an audience." She looked down at the O's Restaurant bag at his feet. "Let me take that for you. The food's over there." She pointed to the far wall near the iPod.

"Not so fast." He held her arm, his fingers branding her with magical heat. "Chase and I studied your drawings and can come up with an added solution."

She refused to let her hope surface, afraid his plan would only backfire. "Business later, okay? Let's have some fun. This is my aunt's night."

Ricardo glanced at Elvira and nodded. "You're right." He picked up the bag and placed his hand at the small of her back, leading her to the table. "I'll walk you over."

He was too quiet. She cast a sidewise glance at him, appreciating the rugged good looks every bit as much as the older women in the studio did. They stepped out of their way, whispering to each other. It looked like she and Cisco were old news.

Julia zeroed in on Chase, standing in the corner next to the food table. Tia Elvira faced him, her arm around a woman with long, blue-black hair.

Chase caught Julia staring and his eyes opened wide, a plea for help if ever she saw one. Julia started for him.

"No way, darlin'. I don't want to miss this." He set the bag at the edge of the table and with a huge grin on his face, sauntered over to Chase. He tipped his hat. "Miss Elvira." He turned to the young woman. "Ma'am."

Elvira introduced the lovely, svelte woman as Lara. Ricardo turned to Chase. "Ms. Elvira wanted you to demonstrate the new salsa move tonight."

A look of utter fear crossed Chase's face. "Hey dude. You've been taking the lessons, not me." He glanced at the Lara.

"You've been to some lessons with me." Ricardo smiled, thoroughly enjoying himself.

"I have two left feet. Except on the football field."

"Miss Elvira, do you have his dance card filled already?"

She beamed. "I'm working on it. Lara is first."

Chase balked. "I was just going to be your sound man. Guard the food table."

Elvira patted his cheek. "All work and no play... except I know you're not a dull boy. I've Googled you."

Julia giggled then immediately tried to put on a straight face. "Sorry, Chase. You're busted. Might as well do your time tonight."

"Busted is right," said Ricardo. "Don't give him too much free time between dances or he'll eat all the food."

Julia elbowed Ricardo. "Chase, I have every confidence you'll glide on the dance floor. And no business talk tonight. This is a party. Try to let loose, move that body and have fun."

Chase let out a breath of relief. "Julia." He stepped around the two women and planted a kiss on her cheek. "Good to see you again. Really."

"Likewise." She wedged herself between Chase and the two women. "Why don't you help Ricardo unload the bag he brought?"

"My pleasure. Ladies." He bowed slightly. "Rick, let's do what the lady asked," he said icily and back-pedaled out of there as fast as his feet would take him.

Chase was giving Ricardo a few choice words, she was sure. His mouth moved silently, a hundred miles a minute. A look of pure amusement lit Ricardo's face. A group of the sixth-grade students swooped down on the two men, and a lot of joking and shoving ensued as they tried to get to the breadsticks first.

Men. They started early. Julia turned her attention back to the two women. "Auntie, what's up?"

"Oh, nothing, *mija*. If Chase stays, he needs to dance. I'm just introducing him to some of my younger students."

"Just introducing…and then you're letting him make his own choices? Right?"

Her aunt let out a deep, martyr-like sigh. She glanced back at Chase and Ricardo, who had inched their way to the table and already held small paper plates filled with food. "Of course."

"Good." Julia turned to Lara. "He'll probably dance with you when he's not backed against the wall."

"I hope so," she said. She smiled and walked off to join a group of women near the front entrance.

Aunt Elvira clapped her hands to get everyone's attention. "Better get started before those two boys eat the food for the entire party," she muttered.

When only a few people stopped their conversations, Julia brought two fingers to her lips and let out a piercing whistle. Then she stepped behind Ricardo to keep from being so conspicuous.

He set down his food, stepped aside, and wrapped an arm around her. "I'm impressed. A not-so-subtle way of getting someone's attention."

"There's a time and a place for everything. Subtle doesn't work tonight."

He leaned down and whispered in her ear, "What would work tonight, darlin'?"

Ah, so he was feeling better now. In the crowded room, he apparently had no qualms about flirting and she liked that. "Use your imagination, 'darlin'.'"

He popped his tongue in his cheek, trying, it seemed, to suppress a smile. It didn't work long. When he slid his hand slowly down her back to the curve of her backside, a flash of pleasure shot through her. His luscious lips curved into a slow smile. She wanted to taste him. He innocently stared straight ahead.

Aunt Elvira's voice drifted around Julia, but she didn't hear a word. How could she concentrate on anything other than the warmth of his big hand? Or the warmth filling her? Two could play his game.

She turned to face him and laid a hand on his chest, pressing hard to feel his heartbeat. It raced as quickly as her own. His smile disappeared, replaced by a look she couldn't read, but it was a look that curled her toes. Everything around them became one big blur.

He placed his hand over hers. "Feel what you do to me, darlin'?"

She swallowed hard. "Then we're even."

"That's good to know." His fingers curled around hers.

Her aunt's voice drifted through her muddled thoughts. "And so, my niece Julia and her dance partner, Ricardo, will lead off the party with the first dance. Let's give them a hand."

Yanked from her reverie, Julia's stomach sank. Clapping and catcalls filled the room, making it grow smaller by the minute.

"I wish I had a camera." Chase pushed Ricardo forward. "What goes around comes around. Ha. Think twice before torturing me next time."

Ricardo dropped his hand from Julia's back. "Is she serious?" His voice nearly cracked.

"Very. We're standing together, we're dancing together. No argument. No turning back. No choice."

He shrugged. "I could think of worse things, darlin'."

"Don't push your luck." She took his hand, leading him onto the dance floor. She shuddered. "I hate center stage when it's not my choice."

She let out a deep breath. "Showtime."

She turned on the charm, smiled, and waved at everyone when all she wanted was to escape to the balcony with Ricardo. *Where did that come from?* No, she was glad for the chaos around them, she tried to convince herself, better until the business plan was complete.

Flashbulbs went off, and she rolled her eyes. "Next time, stand on the opposite side of the room, and keep your hands to yourself, would you? This is probably her attempt at punishing me."

"As I recall, your hands did a little wandering of their own, ma'am. You're as much at fault as I am."

Thankfully, the lights dimmed in the nick of time. Heat rushed to her face. He took a step back from her and raised her hand to his lips.

The fire raged on. It hadn't been a figment of her imagination. Her heart refused to stop its unruly hammering. She was speechless.

"Look, Julia, we might as well make the best out of a bad situation." He glanced around. Singles, couples, and happy, loud children lined the perimeter of the floor, waiting. He saw Don Carlos and waved. He waved back.

"Will she start off with something slow?" he asked hopefully.

"Get ready, Ricardo. This is a party. We're going to kick it until people need to catch their breath."

She slipped into his arms. "Just follow my lead, *querido.*"

"You're leading?"

The mortified look on his face made her laugh. "Don't worry. They won't catch on."

The music blared forth. Her hips automatically started swaying, her dress swishing around her thighs. Her hands felt small in his, and they were warmed instantly. The feeling permeated to the bone. "Got the beat, Ricardo?"

He nodded but kept his eyes glued on her feet. She slipped her hand from his grasp and tilted his chin. "Look at me like you mean it. Trust yourself. Close your eyes if you must. But trust yourself, and trust me."

Trust me, she thought.

He groaned. "You got it, darlin'. Let's go."

"Five, six, seven, and go."

He stepped on her toe right off the bat. "Sorry," he mumbled and started to look down again.

"Ah, ah, ah, Ricardo." She rubbed her hand along his shoulder and laid it to rest on his neck. It was the only natural thing to do. "I've had hundreds of students over the years. You're better than many."

"You're just being nice."

"A rarity around you, I know."

"It's delightful. You're delightful."

She laughed. His body instantly relaxed. His powerful legs pushed against hers and the "quick, quick, slow" glide took on a life of its own.

Elvira clapped. "Everyone dance! Thank you, Julia and Ricardo!"

Julia smiled. "Thank goodness she didn't drag that out."

"That wasn't too painful," Ricardo said. His confidence growing, he finally glanced at Julia and sent her into a dramatic twirl. "How am I doing, teacher?"

"Better. Ricardo, trust yourself. Look at me like you mean..." How many times had she said that phrase to students over the years? She had never wanted it to be truer than at this moment.

He looked at her with eyes that saw through her. A shiver ran through her body. Enemy—opponent—adversary. Her mind screamed out the three logical descriptions befitting Ricardo, the businessman.

But the man standing before her wasn't just a businessman. Her heart didn't listen one bit.

Not when he pulled her closer than the instruction book warranted. Not when his slow drawl pulled her even closer. "I do mean it, darlin'."

And definitely not when he stopped dancing and touched his lips to hers. "Promise me the last dance, too, Julia?"

She wanted to promise more than a dance, but fear at the thought choked her into silence. She nodded and looked down at her unmoving feet. The couples around them spun and whipped, laughed and winked. She wanted a joy like theirs. She wanted it with Ricardo.

The music changed to a soft, slow jazzy tune.

"I thought slow stuff didn't happen 'til later."

"I don't think my aunt had anything to do with this." Julia jerked her had in the direction of the iPod. Chase stood next to it with a big smile on his face.

Julia laughed. Life at this moment was good.

They swayed for minutes in silence, the murmur of voices in the studio playing a steady harmony to the music. She rested her head on Ricardo's chest. His quickened heartbeat was the sweetest music of all.

Then a crash splintered the silence.

A piercing scream chilled Julia to the bone. She jerked out of Ricardo's arms, looking around frantically. "Oh, my God. Grandpa!"

CHAPTER TEN

Ricardo and Julia ran toward the small group huddled by the bathroom door.

"Help me!" Lorenza was banging on the door with all her might. "*Ay, Dios mio,* help me! It's Carlos!"

The house lights flipped on. "Step back, everyone, step back!" Ricardo pushed his way through the crowd. "Give me room. Damn it, give me room."

Lorenza's pounding grew weaker. She looked up at Ricardo, her makeup running in rivulets down her weathered cheeks. "Help me, Ricardo. I can't open the door." Her voice cracked, and fresh tears fell.

He took her raw and bloody fists in his hands. "You did good, Lorenza." He gently kissed her hands and moved her out of the way. Julia wrapped an arm around Lorenza's heaving shoulders.

Chase led Lorenza away. Elvira clung to Julia, frozen a few feet behind Ricardo.

Ricardo jiggled the doorknob. It was heavy brass, the door, panels of solid oak. "Don Carlos, if you can hear me, if you can move, move away from the door."

He heaved back and rammed his shoulder into the door. He tried again. It barely budged.

To get better leverage and more power, he knew he had to use his left shoulder. He sucked in his breath and threw himself against the door. Pain shot through his shoulder like scorching fire.

He took a deep breath and rammed against it again. His bones felt like shattering shards of piercing glass.

He gritted his teeth against the pain. Nausea rose and his vision swam. He staggered back a few steps.

Focus. Focus. He let out a raucous yell and with every ounce of his weight he ran into the door.

It gave. He punched through the indentation, pulled away some splintering wood, and stuck his hand through the small opening. He unlocked the door from the inside and controlled himself, slowly pushing it open.

It opened less than a foot. Ricardo peered in. Don Carlos lay on the floor blocking the way. "No, no, no," Ricardo whispered.

He squeezed in, the door pushing against Don Carlos. Ricardo had already wasted too much time. He fell to his knees next to the unmoving body.

Julia tried to squeeze into the tiny room.

"Get out, Julia! Get some help! Nine-one-one!"

"They're on their way. Let me in, damn it!"

He gently moved Don Carlos's body toward him, knowing he couldn't keep her out. He started CPR. "Help me count, Julia."

She shoved the door open all the way. The fresh air cleared his head. "Elvira! Get them away from the doorway!"

Elvira yelled for them to move.

Julia knelt across from Ricardo. Bringing her hand to her mouth, she shook her head. "Help me or get out, Julia."

"I'm sorry." She carefully lifted her grandpa's glasses from his pale face and began counting.

Ricardo pressed on Don Carlos's chest to Julia's rhythmic counting. He ignored the screaming pain shooting through his shoulder and arm. "Come on, old man. Come on. You're not getting out of this that easily. We have an announcement to make. You're going to be there."

Julia looked at him as if he had sprouted another head. She took her grandpa's limp hand in hers. "Come on, Grandpa. Don't leave me now."

A buzz started in the silent studio. Paramedics raced into the building and glanced into the room. "We'll take over. Good job."

Not good enough, Ricardo thought, looking at the blue tinge around Don Carlos's lips. Damn it, not good enough. He rose and backed out of the room, pulling Julia by the hand.

They stood just outside the doorway, watching IVs and syringes and monitors. The paramedics ripped open Don Carlos's shirt to attach monitors and lifted him onto a gurney.

One paramedic spoke into a radio while the other continued prodding Don Carlos. "Heart attack. He's breathing. Pressure's dropping. Losing color."

They spit out questions left and right. Julia shouted back answers. The medication Don Carlos was on. Other attacks. History.

"We're on our way," the paramedic shouted one last time into the radio.

"We're going with you!" Julia screamed.

"You can't, ma'am. Regulations."

Chase stepped between them. "I'll drive you." He looked at Ricardo. "Both of you. I'll pull the truck up."

Ricardo nodded. The weight on his chest threatened to crush him. Breathing became more difficult every second he looked at Don Carlos's falling blood pressure on the gauge. He saw his father, the way he'd looked just a few years ago, in that hospital bed. The bed that gave him life—and took everything he owned.

They stood on the crowded sidewalk, watching them load Don Carlos into the ambulance. Glancing at Julia's pale face and trembling lips, Ricardo prayed like he had never prayed before.

Tears brimming, Julia's gaze settled on him. The utter despair on her face slashed his heart into shreds.

He wanted to tell her everything would be all right but didn't want to give false hope. He wanted to gather her to him but feared hurting her further. He wanted to promise her no more pain. But more pain was evident.

"I'm so sorry, Julia."

She raised her shaking hand, and with the gentlest touch Ricardo had every known, wiped the dampness from his cheek.

They had whisked Don Carlos to intensive care before Ricardo and Julia had even arrived at Sharp Memorial. Ricardo staggered into the emergency room and clutched his shoulder.

Julia's eyes opened wide. She grabbed him around the waist. "Ay, Montalvo. Why didn't you say anything, *mi corazon?*"

He tried to shrug, but his shoulder refused to cooperate. "Was busy." The words slurred. He licked his lips, wanting to say her name, but his mouth was dry and there seemed to be a disconnect between his brain and actions.

She'd called him *corazón*. That much he could interpret as he closed his eyes and let her soft voice rain over him.

She helped him through the emergency doors and sat him in the first empty seat she could find. At the front desk, she kept glancing back at him, her voice fading in and out like the tide at Mission Beach.

He loved her. He blinked hard, trying to keep her in focus.

With an intern at her side, they brought a wheelchair. "We're going to get you fixed up right now."

"Carlos?" he managed. Panic coursed through him as he tried to sit up straighter. It seemed like hours since he'd been brought to the emergency room. Since they'd heard any word.

The palm of her hand rested on his forehead, then brushed back his hair. "They're taking care of him." Her voice quavered. "By the time they're done with you, we'll know more."

Julia and the intern helped him into the wheelchair. Beads of perspiration trickled down his temples. Julia wiped his face. "Thank you, Ricardo," she whispered and kissed his forehead. "I'm going to run up and see Grandpa, and I'll be back as fast as I can. Sammy will take care of you, okay?"

Don't go, he wanted to shout at her retreating body, but it was all he could do to swallow. *I love you,* he thought, before the pain seared his body one last time and darkness slowly engulfed him.

Family and friends lined the hospital corridor outside intensive care. The vision took Ricardo back to his grandmother's death. His parents had kissed him and his sisters often in those last days spent in the hospital, grim reality striking hard. They had been there for him when their own world crashed down around them. He had vowed never to take someone's love for granted again. But then he had turned and left, too scared and angry to look back. And today, he'd taken for granted the love of another friend.

He didn't intend to make that same mistake again with Julia.

Julia paced at the end of the hallway. Someone had wrapped her in an oversized Chargers' football jacket. The bottom of her party dress showed beneath it. She wore running shoes. Her hair was twisted into a knot at the back of her neck, held there by a yellow pencil. Silky strands fell loosely around her face.

She was the most beautiful vision Ricardo had ever seen.

He walked the gauntlet, clumsily pushing the cart he'd wrangled from the cafeteria with his good arm. It was filled with cups of black coffee, boxed juices, and cans of Pepsi. He stopped every few feet, offering the tired visitors a drink. It was the least he could do.

Arms reached out to him and touched him. Voices he didn't recognize murmured his name over and over. The faces he'd seen a hundred times in the studio or in the neighborhood blurred as he focused on Julia. He mumbled incoherent words, unable to look at anyone else. He left the cart in the middle of the hallway.

He continued toward her, wanting to rip off the sling that held his left arm tight against his chest. The coarse material dug into his neck, immobilized his arm, and slowed his coordination.

Julia turned and looked at him. For a moment, a light in her eyes flickered. With a blink, it disappeared. Her beseeching gaze searched his face and settled on his shoulder.

She took a few steps toward him. "Ricardo, I'm sorry. They told me you'd be downstairs in a couple more hours. I was going back in a while to check on you."

"Once I could sit up and found my hat, I was out of there." His fledgling attempt at humor bombed. She looked at him with vacant eyes, her smile stuck somewhere deep inside her.

With his good arm he drew her close. "You have more important things to worry about."

She rested her head against his chest. He stroked the back of her head, jarring the pencil loose, and it clattered to the floor. Slowly, Julia wrapped her arms around Ricardo's waist and let out a shuddering breath.

"How's he doing?" He wasn't sure he wanted to know.

She lifted her head to look Ricardo in the eyes. "Better, actually. Critical, but stable." She slipped her hand into his. "Come see him."

"I don't think I should. He needs his rest." Ricardo wanted to remember Don Carlos drinking down a cold beer or on the dance floor surrounded by admiring women.

"You saved his life, Montalvo."

"He's not out of the woods yet, Julia."

"The more reason for you to see him now." Her voice remained calm, though her eyes screamed a silent plea.

One look in her eyes and he swallowed down his panic. He squeezed her hand. "Let's do it, then, darlin'."

She led him into the darkened room. Ricardo stopped at the doorway, his feet unwilling to step in farther. Don Carlos looked tiny and frail in the hospital bed. His eyes were closed. His chest rose and fell faster than it should have.

"I don't belong here, Julia," he whispered. He glanced at the IVs hooked up to Don Carlos. His veins stood out on the backs of his hands, folded neatly, as in prayer, on his stomach.

Julia's mother and father had drawn their chairs close to the side of the bed. Her uncle and his wife stood on the opposite side. Elvira stood near the window, staring through the blinds to the street below.

Ricardo stepped back.

"You're his friend," Julia said quietly.

"I don't think that's quite the term your family would impose on me."

Julia squeezed his hand tighter. "Oh, yes, they would." She bit her trembling lips.

He didn't want to face any of them. "I probably caused the heart attack. Some friend."

He'd taken Don Carlos's family and run over them like a bulldozer, all for the sake of a building. In the end, he had been the ruthless monster Julia had believed him to be. Instead of responding in kind, her family had opened their arms and doors to him. They had invited him to be a part of their lives, knowing full well his agenda.

One by one they had opened his heart and eyes to a world beyond business, had made him yearn for the family he only now realized he missed and could not do without. He wanted more than business. He wanted Julia more than anything he could ever remember wanting.

Would she have him? He swallowed the lump in his throat. Hand in hand, they walked to the foot of the bed.

Don Carlos deserved more than respect. Ricardo would do everything in his power to see that he received the best medical attention money could buy. As soon as he was up and around again,

Ricardo would tell him his plans for the studio.

He would clean up the mess he'd made. He'd ask Julia's forgiveness, then leave town. The more space he put between the Rios family and himself, the easier it would be for them to pick up the pieces of their lives again—the pieces he had ripped out from under them.

The thought of leaving Julia pierced him, the pain deeper than any he felt from his shoulder injury.

Her mother rose from the chair, took his face in her hands, and kissed him. "Thank you, Ricardo." Tears streamed down her face.

Julia's father squeezed his shoulder. "She needs a break. Please, take our seats. Take care of Julia."

Marco and his wife followed them with pink pastry boxes stuffed beneath their arms. Ricardo hoped the coffee was still hot for them. Marco patted Ricardo on the back. "He asked for you, son."

Ricardo wanted to bolt. Family, family, family. He'd abandoned one, nearly wrecked another, and yet he knew they'd help him, without hesitation, if he needed them.

Ricardo pulled the chair out for Julia. He eased his hand out of her grasp and leaned down to kiss her cheek, the pain shooting through his shoulder again. The painkillers were fading fast. "I'll be right back, darlin'."

She nodded and scooted her chair closer to the bed. She laid her hand over her grandpa's.

Ricardo walked over to Elvira and placed his hand on her shoulder. "I'm so sorry, Miss Elvira."

She looked up at him with red-rimmed eyes, her tears spilling over. If the earth could open up and swallow him whole, he'd have jumped in headfirst. He hugged her awkwardly, cursing himself for his own stupidity.

Silent sobs wracked her fragile body until he thought she would break. After a few minutes she shuddered to a stop. "Yesterday he told me to make up my mind about the studio," she whispered. "He always worried about me. He said life was short and I'd better do all the things I wanted or I'd run out of time and always wonder 'what if?' He said you were sent from heaven with an opportunity in disguise."

Threatening to take over a family business was a blessing in disguise? Ricardo cursed the old man. He cleared his throat. "He always knew what to say." He glanced at Don Carlos and Julia, who hadn't budged an inch. "We don't need to talk business now."

"I know, Ricardo, but I'm closing up shop anyway. I've always wanted to visit Spain and Greece. It's a good time to do that."

He was speechless. The revised plans, the opportunities. The guilt. "No, Miss Elvira. Please."

"It's time, Ricardo." She patted his cheek. "He said you were a good boy. I firmly believe that, too." Elvira glanced at the hospital bed. "My niece is smitten with you and shaken up about her grandfather. It's not the best negotiating position to be in. You have my word I'll help you all I can. Do what you must do, but don't you dare hurt her." She lifted her chin, just like Julia often did around him, and swiped at the tears on her face.

She left him standing there speechless and hugged Julia, pulling her close enough so that their cheeks touched.

Don Carlos stirred. Julia gasped. Elvira kissed him and hurried from the room to call the others. Julia rose and gently stroked a pattern on his forehead, easing the furrow that appeared there.

"*Chiquita.*" Don Carlos licked his chapped lips. His eyelids twitched, but he didn't open his eyes.

"Shhh, Grandpa."

"Ricardo?" He seemed to swallow with great difficulty.

"I'm right here, Don Carlos." Ricardo reached for the half-full glass of water on the nightstand but thought better of it. He picked out an ice cube and rubbed it over Don Carlos's lips.

"Good. You're together." A tear trickled out of the side of his closed eye, across his temple, and into his hair. "Wish I could see you together. Can't see."

His voice caught and he coughed. His face scrunched against the spasms of pain that must have shot through him.

"You can see us tomorrow, Grandpa," she crooned. "Just get some rest."

Ricardo put down the ice cube and looked at Julia in wonder. Her voice was as comforting as a lullaby, but tears drenched her cheeks, falling from her chin onto the white sheet covering Don Carlos.

"Your grandma is happy, *Chiquita.* He's the one." He sucked in his breath and let it out slowly. "Ricardo, take good care of my baby."

Sweat covered Ricardo's palms and ran in rivulets down his back. He had to say something, anything that would turn the tide. "Old man, you can't go anywhere yet. You have to be at our wedding."

The corners of Don Carlos's lips turned upward into a sad smile. He groped for Julia's hand. Ricardo covered both of theirs with his own.

Julia leaned into Ricardo. Their combined heat had to warm Don Carlos's hands and feet. If it could be that simple, Ricardo thought, he'd have started hours ago.

The monitor beeped wildly and the green line went flat.

CHAPTER ELEVEN

"How long have they been in there?" Ricardo stopped pacing and banged his fist on the wall, making everyone around him jump. "Sorry," he mumbled.

Julia doubted he was. She turned away from him and wished for a moment that she could do the same. She looked out the lone window, fiddling with the cross on her necklace. "They said bypass surgery can last up to ten hours."

She surprised herself at the ability to remember that fact and other tidbits that flowed in and out of her consciousness. Every face, every word uttered, every excruciating minute she had sat in the chair next to Grandpa's bed was a blur. She knew that after Ricardo had been released, he had stayed beside her, had held her, had spoken to her grandpa. Some lame thing about a wedding that actually made Grandpa smile.

Ricardo had comforted her. Right now, he unnerved her.

She rubbed the back of her neck. Her eyes burned unmercifully, and a fresh deluge of tears threatened to start again if someone so much as poked her. She was tired right down to the marrow, an ache that went far beyond anything she'd ever known.

Pounding on the soda machine startled her. "Montalvo! They're going to throw you out of here. Get a grip."

His gaze darted back and forth with the wild-eyed look of a desperate, explosive man. He turned his attention back to the machine and pounded again, his wrapped left arm looking like a broken wing.

He'd been there for her, but who had been there for him? She looked across the crowded room at Chase. He shrugged, the vacant look in his eyes filling with his own demons.

Julia walked to Ricardo and placed her hand in the middle of his back. She trailed her hand up and down the length of it, then pressed more firmly against his tightly strung muscles. "Come sit with me, Montalvo."

He leaned his hand on the machine, pulling his arm taut, and dropped his head onto his upper arm. "You don't want to sit next to me." He slurred his words. "I'm bad luck."

Julia figured the fatigue had finally settled in. She rubbed his back again. "Don't talk like that. There's no one else I'd rather sit next to."

He turned to her. His dark eyes, like bottomless pools, drew her into a world she wasn't sure she wanted to enter. They searched her face for some kind of answer she couldn't possibly give.

His eyes hardened. "Well then, darlin', I feel sorry for you."

Heat rose to her face and before she could stop herself, the tears spilled over. What had gotten into him? "You should just stop feeling sorry for yourself, Montalvo."

His head jerked up. He looked at her as if for the fist time. "Julia, I'm sorry. I'm sorry. How many times will I need to keep on saying that?"

"You've said it enough." She hiccoughed. "Damn it, Montalvo, I'm so tired of crying. And tired of your apologies. You have nothing to do with Grandpa's condition."

"I'm sor... come here." He turned around and reached for her.

"No." She sniffled like a child. "Deal with your guilt on your own time. I know that's what you're fighting but it'll be there in the morning, believe me, and I don't want to be there when you come head to head with it."

"Please, Julia. I'm sorry."

There was that drawl again, curling around her like a warm blanket. She wanted to snuggle against it and fall asleep for days and wake up with this nightmare well behind her. "No," she whispered, but her feet had a will of their own.

He led her by the hand to the nearest empty chair. He sat down and pulled her into his lap. He shifted her and moaned.

She bolted upright. "Your shoulder."

"It's fine." He drew her to his chest and rested his chin on the top of her head. "Julia, if I had to do this all over again, I would never drag you or your family through it," he whispered for her ears only. "You say I saved your grandpa's life? Well, darlin', you all saved mine."

His fingers hung from the sling and grazed her thigh, the warmth of his touch seeping into her tired, aching bones. "We have to fix everything. We will fix everything."

She halfway believed him. She clung to the front of his shirt, wet from her tears. She shifted into a more comfortable position, curling against his hard, sturdy body. He held her tight against him and she believed, in that instant, she could find the answers she'd been seeking right there in his arms.

His voice droned over her like the lazy buzz of honeybees in summer. His soft and steady breathing calmed her own. Fighting the makeshift lullaby as long as she could, she finally gave in and allowed her eyes to flutter closed.

The buzz grew louder and rolled over Julia. She knew she was awake but her body refused to accept that fact. Slowly, she opened her eyes one at a time.

Francisco stood in the doorway with a huge grin on his face. "Hey, everybody. I'm the bearer of good news. Carlos is in recovery and doing fine."

A cheer went up from the crowd and Montalvo jerked awake, nearly sending Julia crashing to the floor. He winced at the pain the sudden movement had caused his shoulder and threw his good arm around her, as if to protect her. "What the...?"

He looked around wildly until his gaze fell on Francisco. Their eyes locked. The temperature in the room dropped a few notches, and Julia shuddered. With that fixed, icy stare, Ricardo looked downright scary. She could see how ominous he'd be on the football field or in intense negotiations. Francisco stayed formidably cool and she knew he could easily confront any political opponent in any type of debate.

If she hadn't been in the middle, she would have stepped aside and watched the fireworks.

"What a nightmare way to wake up," mumbled Ricardo. "What did you ever see in that guy?"

She gave Francisco the once-over. Freshly shaved and creased to perfection, he was spotless. He worked the room, his handshakes firm, his smile warm, his words comforting. If he had been anyone else, she would have thought him a typically smooth politician. At least here, in this room, he was genuine and sincere. She had no doubt about that.

"He's a good man. My friend. Like family." And in that moment, she knew it to be true.

She ventured a glance at the scowling Ricardo. Could she convince him that Francisco posed no threat?

Ricardo stroked her thigh absentmindedly, never taking his gaze off Francisco. "Smooth politician. Lesson number one: Work that room." He turned to Julia. "Wait a second—he said your grandpa was in recovery."

The news finally sank in. Julia jumped from Ricardo's lap. "Cisco!" she yelled.

"Are you sure about Grandpa?" She rose and smoothed her dress, then ran a hand through her tangled hair.

Francisco approached them. "The doctor came by, but since you were sleeping, I intercepted him."

"Always looking for that opportunity for center stage," Ricardo mumbled. "Don't stand so close, Valdez, you're blinding me."

He laughed heartily. "Good morning to you, too, Montalvo. It's a good day."

Ricardo shook his outstretched hand. "It could have been until you walked in." He smiled wide.

"Actually, I thought the same when you were the first person I saw when I walked in here."

Julia let out an exasperated sigh. "A time and a place, guys. This is not it." She clenched her teeth until they hurt.

Next to Francisco, Ricardo, in his rumpled clothes, tousled hair, and arm hanging from the sling, looked like some defensive line had just put him through the wringer. She rather liked that contrast between the two, but at this moment, she didn't like either one of them very much.

"You took the news but didn't bother to wake me?" Julia fought to control her voice. "And you"—she turned to face

Ricardo—"can only think of cutting Cisco down?"

Both men turned to look at her as if she'd spoken an alien tongue. The room turned silent.

"We have been here all night worried sick, waiting for some word, and you come waltzing in, and *only* when you're good and ready, decide to tell me about my grandfather's condition? What's with that, Cisco?"

"I'm sorry. I wasn't thinking. I just thought I could spare you..."

"You thought nothing but being center stage, like Ricardo said. Now if you'll excuse me, I have my grandpa to tend to."

Ricardo stepped forward. "I'll come with you."

She shook his hand off her arm. "No. Just go ahead with the knock-down-drag-out you guys are on the verge of having and get it over with. I'm tired and have more important things to do."

She pushed her way past them, suddenly aware of her outrageous attire. The running shoes, the Chargers' jacket, her party dress. The makeshift outfit reflected the tornado of chaos inside her. Heaven help them if they got in her way with any more of their macho nonsense.

Julia hurried to the foot of Grandpa's bed and said a quick prayer of thanks. He was breathing normally and his color had returned. Her parents, Aunt Elvira, Uncle Marco, and his wife looked up at her, relief evident in their tentative smiles.

She came around and kissed everyone. She leaned over Grandpa and kissed him gently on the forehead. She touched his soft face with the tips of her fingers, following the path of the many wrinkles and laugh lines as if they were leading her to a treasure.

It wasn't her imagination. His face relaxed. In that moment, she knew she'd found that treasure. He'd be coming home.

Walkie-talkie in hand, Ricardo stood in front of the wide double doors of his restaurant. Only when he spotted Chase in Elvira's studio did he resume his pacing. "Everything under control there, Chase? Don Carlos will be here soon."

The airwaves cackled. Chase stood in the doorway of the studio and waved. "If you use that walkie-talkie to check up on me one more time, I'm tossing mine out the window. Chill out, dude."

"All right, all right. I can take a hint."

"I'm setting my talkie down so I can rearrange things." Chase chuckled and waved one more time.

"Rearrange things?"

The line went dead.

All right, so he was being too detail-oriented. He wanted to pull the surprise off for Don Carlos's homecoming without a hitch. It had been way too long since he'd seen any kind of activity in the studio. The neighborhood clan had practically deserted it since Carlos's near-collision with "the big one" and had opted to visit the hospital daily, for hours on end. Swept along with the emotional tide, he had been there as much as he could.

He glanced at his completed restaurant and then at the studio. Two incredible worlds he was lucky to be a part of.

The studio had become his haven, the people there, his friends. It was a life he had never expected to find and had definitely not appreciated. He missed the liveliness of the studio—the music pumping life into him, the sweet-voiced instructions from Elvira, the feeling it gave him of home.

Mostly, he missed having Julia around since she'd wound up the ad campaign and dance lessons—especially the way she felt in his arms, the way he sometimes caught her looking at him. It was the kind of look that could make any man back into a *saguaro* cactus and never even feel it.

Hell, he drove her crazy, too, but wasn't quite sure if it was a good kind of crazy. He knew he sometimes acted a bit on the hot-headed side, bringing out all the macho behavior she barely tolerated.

All in all, it was a challenge to be around Julia, and he'd told her as much. Then he'd made her smile when he said how much he loved a challenge.

Julia came around the corner in the blue van he'd rented for her. It didn't have quite the same effect as her red Mustang but she could make anything look like a million bucks.

He grabbed the walkie-talkie. "They're here. Get ready."

"Ten-four," Chase answered. "Hey, that sounds great—official," he said, with sudden realization. "Ten-four, good buddy."

"Chase, get in position, for crying out loud."

"Ten-four." The line went dead again, and movement inside the studio ceased.

He set the walkie-talkie on the wooden bench by the door. The bench had been a gift from Marco, made by the same woodworker who had created the one that sat in front of his *panaderia*.

Julia pulled open the sliding doors of the van and started pulling out a wheelchair.

Ricardo ran toward her. "Julia! Let me help you with that."

Her face lit up like a wonderful blossom, nearly making him falter. "Ricardo! Thanks for coming."

"Wouldn't miss it for the world." With one hand, he grabbed the wheelchair and set it up, locking its brakes.

She gently touched his sling. "How're you doing?"

Her vibrant smile made him wish for things he had once thought were out of his reach. "Better every day." He pulled her close. "I've missed that."

She wrapped her arms around his waist. "What's 'that'?"

"Your smile, darlin'."

She sighed and her body relaxed. "Seems like the worst is over."

"Hey!" A cane rapped on the door. "Are you two done? It's hot in here."

"Don Carlos—I see you're back to normal." Ricardo chuckled and stepped away from Julia to help him out of the van.

"It feels good to be home." Don Carlos shuffled to the edge of the van and put a shaky arm around Ricardo's neck.

Ricardo easily lifted Don Carlos and gently set him in the wheelchair while Julia held it steady. Don Carlos looked around, the soft breeze ruffling his hair.

"The studio's too quiet, but it looks wonderful." He pointed with his cane toward Ricky's. "So does your restaurant from this angle, son."

"Wait until you see the finalized plans, Don Carlos." He and Chase had worked with a new landscape designer to bring Julia's first drawings to life.

"I'm sure they'll be a work of art."

"I hope all of you think so." He could hardly wait to see the look on Julia's face when he brought out the modified plans tonight.

Cobblestone walkways and bridges linking the studio and various other businesses to the restaurant would replace the asphalt. Sod would be laid everywhere, for the immediate, necessary green to give the place life. Splashes of color would come from the tons of flowerbeds they'd planned for—with roses, jasmine and lilac, magnolias, verbena and star lilies. The scent of those flowers had permeated the air so intensely in his office, it had to be a sign of some sort. He'd jumped at the idea of including them in the landscaping. Vines of wisteria and bougainvillea would lace the columns and trellises on the buildings.

He stepped behind the wheelchair. "Please, allow me, darlin'. If you could get the door."

"What are you up to?" she whispered as she tried slipping around him.

He wasn't about to let her squeeze past him that quickly. He pressed his body against hers, blocking her way.

"Well?" she whispered, not at all flustered by their stance. Her raised eyebrows taunted him even further.

"Just a little surprise." He reluctantly let her pass.

"Uh-oh. You don't know the meaning of little. Just make sure I'm out of the vicinity when you spring this little surprise." She winked at him and gave him her thousand-watt smile, revving him up.

"Surprise? What surprise?" The impatience in Don Carlos's voice was more than apparent. "Never mind, let's get a move on. Elvira's probably worried sick."

Ricardo pushed the wheelchair through the front door Julia held open and walked through the lobby to the studio.

"Surprise!"

Don Carlos was startled, and then a smile spread across his face.

Family and friends filled the room. A variety of pastries, heaping bowls of rice and beans, trays of enchiladas and *carne asada* and stacks of tortillas filled the two tables along the far wall. The scent was absolutely heavenly.

Hanging from the ceiling was a huge banner reading *Welcome Home, Don Carlos!* Chase flipped on the music but kept it at a respectable decibel level. Ricardo gave him a thumbs-up.

Everyone rushed toward Don Carlos, jabbering a hundred miles a minute.

"Thank you, thank you," he whispered, but his voice was drowned out. Placing a hand on Don Carlos's shoulder, Ricardo leaned close to his ear. "Do you want to say something or forever hold your peace?"

"I'd like to say something." He covered Ricardo's hand with his own. "Don't leave."

Ricardo swallowed hard. "I won't, old man. You know that." Afraid to yell or whistle while standing close to Don Carlos, he gestured to Julia to give her piercing whistle.

She did. The chatter dwindled and finally stopped. All eyes were riveted on Don Carlos.

"You almost gave me a heart attack," he said. The crowd stood, stunned. Don Carlos laughed. "I'm joking."

Breaking the ice, everyone laughed with him. Don Carlos held up his hands. "You are all the reason I decided to stay. It was you who brought me home. I missed all of you." His voice broke.

Ricardo blinked hard, suddenly not liking where he stood. Being in the spotlight with the man who had made him take a good, hard look at his way of life was sobering. Everyone was bound to see right through his façade, but he was far from ready to make any emotional revelations in public.

"I've lived a long, full, and wonderful life and still find life too short. Today I'm surrounded by the only things that matter—my family and friends."

He reached out his hand. "Julia, Elvira, Maria, Marco, your wives and husbands. And those who will always be like family—Ricardo, Francisco, Chase— come here." They gathered around him. "If there's any advice I can give, it's don't waste a precious minute. Do what you've always wanted to do, surround yourself with those that mean the most to you."

He took off his glasses and laid them on his lap. He covered his eyes with a shaky hand, the tears flowing despite his best efforts.

Flashbulbs went off. Ricardo had befriended one of the sixth-graders and hired him to take photos of the celebration.

Francisco stepped forward, and for once, Ricardo was glad he did. "Don Carlos, I can't tell you how glad we are to have you home. This is definitely a day of new beginnings."

Ricardo risked a glance at Julia. For once in his life he was speechless, unable to express his love not only for this woman but for her generous, loving family.

Tears streamed down Julia's cheeks, but she held his gaze. He took her outstretched hand. "Dance with me later?" he asked, wiping the tears from her face.

She nodded.

Elvira slipped away from the crowd for a moment before returning with a rolled sheet of paper bound by a rubber band. She kissed Don Carlos and stood so close to him that her leg touched his wheelchair. "I'd like to say something."

Chase turned down the music. Perfectly poised, Elvira turned to face the larger group of friends. "These last few weeks, my father taught me many, many lessons."

She fiddled with the paper, rolling it back and forth between her hands. "I'm taking Dad's words to heart, to do the things I've always wanted to do before time slips away."

A buzz started through the crowd. Heads bobbed up and down in understanding.

"I'm going to travel to Spain and Greece." She tilted her chin, her youthful, hardly lined face serene. Her bottom lip quivered.

Ricardo's blood ran cold. "No."

She couldn't do this now. He was going to make everything right. He tried to yank his hand from Julia's but she clung tighter, holding him back so Elvira could finish.

"At the end of the month, when I hope my father will be better, I'm closing down Elvira's Dance Studio so I can travel."

A gasp went up from the crowd. She held up her hand holding the white paper to get their attention, but to Ricardo, it looked like a flag of surrender.

"I love you all. You are my life and I will miss this place, but alas, it is only a building."

Tears, tears, everywhere tears, and Ricardo felt as if he were drowning. It was more than a building. Could they see through their tears the beast he had been, that he had caused this painful decision?

Her voice quavered unashamedly. "I'll always dance with you here." She pointed to her heart. "Tonight, I need you to be happy for me that my father is with us again. As Cisco said, let's make this a day of beginnings, a celebration we all need very much. Tonight we will dance here"— she spread out her arms like wings— "Like we've never danced before. Chase, the music."

A distraught Chase merely nodded and cranked up the music a notch.

The shock slowly wore off the guests. Lorenza walked up to Elvira and gave her a bear hug. "It's about time, *mija*."

"You have to come with me."

"I thought you'd never ask. Those matadors better watch out."

Lorenza pressed her cheek to Don Carlos's cheek. "Hurry up and get on your feet before the end of the month, Carlos. I want to dance with you one more time in this studio."

Don Carlos laughed and kissed her. "That's my goal, Lorenza. I'll sweep you off your feet."

"You'd better. No excuses."

She turned to Ricardo. "Why are you looking so shell-shocked? It was time. Everything will work out fine." She patted his chest and walked over, grabbing an unsuspecting gentleman and pulling him to the center of the dance floor.

The celebration picked up. When the crowd dispersed to talk to Don Carlos, Elvira walked over to Ricardo.

"Miss Elvira, I'm so sorry."

"We've gone through this before, Ricardo. No more apologies. I really, really want to see Spain." She placed the white sheet in his hand and curled his fingers over it. "This is the lease for the building. You can work out the details with Julia. It's yours to do with what you will."

She patted his cheek. "You are a good man. Whatever you do, do it wisely and with heart." She kissed Julia, then turned and walked toward the hub of people on the other side of the room.

He turned to Julia, desperation filling him. "Please, darlin', talk her out of this."

Julia bit her lip and shook her head. "She's made up her mind, Montalvo. If I could, believe me, I would."

The sadness in her eyes was too much for him to take. He had pushed her family against the wall until they had no other recourse. It was what he had wanted, wasn't it?—to win the studio and make it into a parking lot? Now that it was his, it was a shallow victory—hell, no victory at all.

He shifted the paper into his almost useless hand and touched her cheek. How would Julia ever want him after he'd caused her family such sorrow? He'd let her down, let them all down.

The music that had brought him joy by bringing Julia comfortably into his arms became unbearably loud. He dropped his hand from her soft skin and backed away.

"I'm sorry, Julia." He wadded up the paper in his clenched fist and stalked from the studio, ignoring the echoes of his name.

Ricardo sat in the middle of the empty dance floor in his restaurant on one not-so-cozy barstool. He made a note to buy more comfortable ones. He stroked his chin, over and over again, as if he could magically rub answers right out of it like a genie from a bottle.

He looked around. Julia had been his genie, turning the restaurant design into one of the best in his chain. She had worked miracles in bringing the flavor of Old Town to the place, helping it to blend in. The advertising campaign was both aggressive and appealing.

Hell, who was he trying to kid? The restaurant meant nothing without Julia. Julia had made wishes he hadn't ever dared whisper come true. Why on God's green earth would she hang around if he drove her family away?

He couldn't imagine his life without her now. There would be no satisfaction in opening the restaurant if he couldn't share it with her.

"Dollar for your thoughts." Julia's voice wafted out to him on the strains of the salsa tune bellowing from her aunt's studio. She stood in the doorway separating the restaurant from the dance club. As she neared him, her face, fresh with makeup, looked satiny smooth. All evidence of her earlier tears had disappeared, leaving her eyes bright and stunning.

He swallowed hard at what she reduced him to. He didn't take any offense to it, but it would take some getting used to. "Some things you just can't put a price on now can you, darlin'?"

"Not the things that matter." She walked up behind him and firmly massaged his neck and between his shoulder blades. "Do you want to talk about it?"

"Damage has already been done." Magic in her fingertips, magic in her kiss. He rolled his shoulders but nothing would loosen the knots there or the one tying up his insides.

"Ricardo, come back to the party. Everyone's waiting for you." She cupped her hand around the back of his neck and moved to stand in front of him. "Everything works out for a reason. Chase is watching Grandpa, but I can't spare more than a few minutes."

Her lips looked soft, tinted a color reminding him of red, juicy plums. If he could just taste her bottom lip, he'd head back to Texas knowing he'd tasted heaven. "We should be getting him home soon."

"There's time. Everyone is celebrating. We want you there too."

He looked into her eyes. "Do you really want me there, Julia?"

She rested her forehead against his, her breath soft and easy, almost forgiving. *"Mi corazón,* I want you there, but you have to get past your guilt and your demons to make room for me."

"I can't do that unless you forgive me first." He gritted his teeth. "Can you forgive me for all I've done to your family?"

"It wasn't all you, Ricardo. You didn't *do* anything to us. We had the choice of how we'd react to your proposal."

He ripped off the sling, wincing as he lifted his hands to her shoulders. Her facial reaction would clearly give the answer, whether he wanted to know the truth or not. "Can you forgive me for barging in like some greedy lunatic, disrupting your lives, causing grief?"

For an instant, she dropped her gaze. "I don't know. I don't know." She looked him squarely in the eye. "All I know is I love you."

He studied her face, agony and despair taking root, emotions that should never have been there. The knot in his stomach tightened unrelentingly. "Love's not always enough."

She shook her head. "No, it's not. We have some things to work through. I need to see how Auntie and Grandpa will do." She slipped his hands from her shoulders and sighed.

If he kissed her, he'd keep her from saying more of what he didn't want to hear. He hesitated a second too long.

She locked her fingers with his. "Nothing can happen until you deal with your demons, and I guess I have to deal with mine."

He pulled his left hand away to stroke the curve of her face, to tilt the chin that had defied him countless times over the last few months. "Then I have to go back home, Julia."

Her body tensed beneath his fingers. "Texas? After all this, you still consider it home, or is it just a place you can run away to?"

"I'm not running. I'm just..." *Running,* he thought miserably. But he also knew he had to make things right with his own family. And maybe then he'd figure out how to make things right with the Rios family. "I love you, Julia."

"I know." She kissed him gently on the lips and started for the door. "Do what you have to do," she whispered. "You'll always know where to find me."

CHAPTER TWELVE

The foreman hopped off his rig and sauntered over to Ricardo. "Excuse me, sir."

Ricardo threw him a cursory glare and went back to the business of watching Elvira's place. "What's up?"

"Mr. Montalvo, my crew's been sitting idle for three days now and I'm just wondering how soon you'll want us to demolish the building so that I can schedule the rest of the week."

Ricardo propped his foot on the railing and leaned on his leg, never taking eyes off the studio. "I'm paying you twice the going rate. Do you think you could come up with some creative way of fighting your boredom?"

The man didn't flinch. "Yessir, but we have other customers, too, sir."

Ricardo lifted the mirror-framed sunglasses to the top of his bare head. "I'll let you know by this evening. Is that soon enough?"

"Yessir." He turned to walk away.

"Wait a minute." He pushed away from the railing and reached inside the front door. He grabbed several of the dozen pastry boxes filled with Marco's *pan dulce*. "I'm sorry. It's been a hell of a month. This is for your crew—the best Mexican sweet bread in town, and it comes from right across the street."

He pointed to an aluminum-siding shed at the back and to the right of the restaurant. "There's a fridge in there stocked with sodas and water. Help yourselves. It's going to be a hot one today."

"Thanks, Mr. Montalvo."

He saluted the foreman half-heartedly. He needed to catch Elvira leaving today. The last few days, she'd evaded him like the plague. If he couldn't convince her to stay, he at least wanted to run a contingency plan by her. She just had to stop avoiding him.

She walked out of the door in a bright, flowery dress and high heels and set down a small suitcase and large poster board against the building. From her purse she pulled out keys and locked the door. She dropped them back into her purse and pulled out a roll of tape.

She deftly hung the poster board and stepped back to stare at it. She hugged herself for a moment, made the sign of the cross, and picked up her suitcase.

Ricardo quickened his pace, not wanting to run for fear he'd scare her off again. As she turned the corner he glanced at the poster board. *Closed for Business,* it read.

Panic rose in his throat. "Miss Elvira, wait!"

She turned to face him and took a deep breath before she spoke. "Honey, I need to take care of my travel plans and other business before my trip."

"I've thought of another way to keep the studio in the family." Gone was the cool business façade of conquer 'em and leave 'em in the dust. He'd get down on his knees to prompt her to listen and play along.

"You'll need these, then." She yanked the keys from her purse again and placed them in his hand.

"That's not what I came here for. Five minutes is all I'm asking."

She covered his clenched hand with her own. "Julia's miserable. Dad misses his dance lessons."

Ricardo didn't trust himself to speak. All week, the office had rained floral-scented messages on him that he couldn't even begin to decipher, and he knew he couldn't make the wrong business decision again.

Her voice reverted to its sing-song lilt, and she linked her arm with his. "I'll give you ten. Why don't you tell me your plan over a cup of coffee?"

Ricardo paced the office, the thought of seeing Julia again making his blood race. The days apart had been pure torture. Everyone was avoiding him, even Don Carlos. Chase had remained by his side, though he probably wanted to bolt by now, too. "Do you think we can pull this off?"

"What kind of question is that? Of course we can." Chase slapped Ricardo on the back. "Your idea's brilliant. I knew you'd make me proud."

"I'm not doing this for you." He peered out from the blinds for the hundredth time.

"A little tact wouldn't hurt, dude. Julia have any idea?"

"None. I told her I just wanted to finalize the hype for Salsa Night for the grand opening of the restaurant. It's only a week away, so timing's on our side." He started pacing again, slapping his Stetson against his thigh every few steps.

"You're driving me crazy, Rick. If you don't sit your butt down, I'm going to hog-tie you to your chair." He whipped a lasso out of the bottom desk drawer and slapped it against his palm. "Go back to your office and I'll let her in. Sheesh. Control, man."

"I'm in complete control." He shoved the Stetson onto his head and walked past Chase. "I can take a hint. I have to get some work done anyway."

He sprawled into his chair and spun it around several times, work the furthest thing from his mind. He glanced at the shirt-size box near his feet and the bigger box stuffed underneath his desk and patted his shirt pocket.

The sound-bite for the commercial was already pulled on his tablet. The layout of the timed advertisement frames were spread out in the middle of his desk, looking like trumped-up comic strips. He wanted everything to look official, although he didn't want to think he'd have to resort to protocol.

"You wanted to see me?" Julia's throaty voice knocked every one of his opening lines right out of his head.

"Damn straight I wanted to see you, darlin'." He'd never been more sure of anything in his life—until he saw the guarded look in her eyes. "I mean, please come in and have a seat. We need to talk about opening night." *Control, man.*

She walked in without another word and sat in the seat across from his. "Is there a problem?"

"No." He came around his desk and sat on the edge nearest her. She crossed her long legs and gripped the armrests, her bright red nail polish mesmerizing him. He cleared his throat. "I wondered if you'd be interested in giving dance lessons as a promotion for Salsa Night on a weekly basis after we open up shop."

"Me? Where, pray tell?"

"Did you notice that the crews were gone today?"

"I...no." She shifted in her seat.

"I'd like to keep the studio open."

Her voice hardened, her gaze grew wary. "Please don't waste my time."

"I'm not. We're keeping the studio intact, where it is, using your plans to link it to The Ranch in Old Town."

"I don't know what to say. Thank you." Julia swallowed hard. "But it won't be the same without my aunt to run the show."

"True. She's an icon. So we have to work around that so the studio stays busy. We need to advertise it better."

"I can do that. Do you have any questions about the advertising for it or The Ranch?"

"None whatsoever. You're the expert there. I'll leave that in your hands." He dropped on one knee. "I do have another question for you, though."

"Ricardo..." She clasped her hands and brought them to her lips.

"Julia, I don't want to live the rest of my life without you, darlin'. I want to dance with you—every first dance and every last dance, and I promise I'll keep taking lessons so that someday I'll hardly step on your toes at all."

Her mouth dropped open and she laid her hand on his cheek. "What's your question, Montalvo?" she whispered. "Spit it out or forever hold your peace."

"You know what I want."

She nodded. "Probably exactly what I want."

He dropped to one knee and held both her hands in his. "Will you marry me, Julia?"

She took his face in her hands and kissed him full on the mouth. The exquisite taste of Julia. He fumbled in his pocket and pulled out the blue velvet box.

He reluctantly pulled away from her. "Is that a yes?" he asked, never assuming anything where Julia was concerned.

They twined fingers. The scent of roses, wisteria, and several other unidentifiable flowers blended together in the office, simultaneously strong and sensual and perfectly right.

"That's a definite yes, Montalvo. Why did you wait so long?"

"I learn the hard way sometimes." He flipped open the box and took out an antique Marquis diamond ring that had belonged to his grandmother. He slipped it onto Julia's finger. "We're official, darlin'. Can we just skip ahead to the wedding night?"

"No, we cannot." She laughed that silvery laugh he loved and kissed him again.

"Well, then, I'd like to skip ahead to opening a couple of wedding presents. Chase?"

"At your service." On cue, Chase wheeled in a huge cart with three tiers, two filled with champagne flutes, the other with ice buckets containing ice and dark-green bottles of champagne.

"This is an awful lot of champagne for three people," Julia said and stood with her arms crossed.

Chase whipped a white napkin over his forearm. He adopted an English accent. "Then, my dear, why don't we have a celebration?"

"Surprise!" The clan followed him into the room, led by Julia's parents, grandfather, and Elvira.

Julia wrapped her arms around Ricardo's neck. "I love you so much, Montalvo." They kissed, ignoring the catcalls and whistles.

Chase busied himself with pouring champagne. They passed the glasses around quickly until everyone had one. He held up his own.

"A toast. To two of the most stubborn people I've ever known."

Laughter trickled into the room. *"Salud!"*

Julia and Ricardo tapped their glasses together and drank the fruity champagne. He kissed her solid, not in the least intimidated by the family. *The family!*

"I have someone I want you to meet," he whispered to Julia. He took her by the hand until they stood in front of a tall couple, he made more so by his Stetson. "Mom, Dad, this is Julia. Julia, Jess and Lupe Montalvo."

His mom reached for both her hands. "So you're the one. I hope you'll be as happy as we've been. " Her dark eyes looked at Julia warmly and relief spread through him.

"Thank you." Julia leaned in and hugged her.

His dad stepped forward. "So you're the one. My son's a good man. I'm glad you're giving him a chance. It looks like he hit the jackpot with you and your family. It feels like home."

"Thank you. He feels like home to me." Julia smiled and turned to Ricardo. "Wow, you look just like him."

Ricardo took a good look at his dad. He supposed so. Just an inch shorter than Ricardo, he'd always been formidable looking when they were growing up. Until he and his brothers had caught up to him in height and bulk, he'd towered over them and while in uniform you couldn't help but nod and say, "Yes, sir."

Underneath the rigid posture learned from time in the military, he was a man with strong family values and an unparalleled work ethic, someone Ricardo wanted to emulate. What mattered now weren't his looks or posture. It was the simple fact that his dad looked healthy and strong and without the creases of worry on his forehead, a far cry from a year ago.

"I take that as a compliment though I think his mother has all the good genes," he said.

Chase wheeled Don Carlos over to them. Chase hugged Julia tight and kissed her. He turned to Ricardo, hugged him, and whispered, "The sooner you let her open the presents, the sooner we can be out of here and you can carry on, dude."

"Right. Excuse me everyone." Ricardo raced behind his desk and brought out the gifts. "Have a seat, darlin'." He handed her the smaller box first.

She looked around at her family. "I love you all."

"Ay, *Chiquita,* no more suspense." Her grandfather's eyes twinkled merrily.

She grabbed his hand and kissed it before she started pulling off the white satin ribbon from the wedding paper. She lifted the lid off the box and gingerly pulled back the tissue paper.

She covered her mouth with her hands, the silence in the room growing heavy. She stared at Ricardo, her large eyes filling with tears.

Lorenza's voice boomed over all of them. "We're getting old here, Julia."

Julia waved and pulled out a frame. Her family seemed to gasp in one collective breath as they read over her shoulder.

"We can't see over here, kiddo," Lorenza complained. "What is it?"

Julia handed the box to her mother and passed the frame on to her grandfather. She stood and faced her friends. "It's the lease for the studio. And it's now in my name."

"Ahh." The entire group nodded in understanding and began clapping.

She turned to Elvira. "Auntie, what..."

Elvira hugged Julia. "It was Ricardo's idea, but it comes with my full blessing. I should have thought of it years ago."

"Thank you. I'm so honored."

"No. Thank *you*." Elvira stepped back with the rest of the family. "Now I'll really be able to enjoy my travels, knowing the studio is in great hands."

Julia kissed Ricardo again. "I don't know what to say."

"It's okay, darlin'." He touched the strand of hair falling across her cheek. "Just open the next one."

She set the box on the desk between them and opened it. She cried out in delight and grabbed the heavy wooden plaque from the box. It was another sign, hand-painted, a smaller duplicate of Elvira's sign hanging from the shop's awning, save for one small difference.

Julia held it over her head and turned slowly so that everyone could read it. Her smile was radiant, the tears were of joy, her kiss was tender and full of promise. Ricardo's chest puffed up to grand proportions when he glanced at the plaque.

Painted vines of bougainvillea decorated the perimeter of the sign. In beautiful calligraphy was written *Elvira and Julia's Dance Studio.*

The grand opening of The Ranch in Old Town went off without a hitch. Media roamed, guests were happy, the bold were already dancing. Julia had been at his side, gracious and beautiful, and he couldn't remember a happier time.

He asked the hostess to cover the door. Jumping over the railing, he headed for the studio.

Ricardo leaned on the door jamb and watched Julia in her short purple dress, not looking much different from the first time he'd laid eyes on her in that very room. His physical reaction to her hadn't changed either. He found it impossible to control his lust for her these days.

A country-western tune belted out of the iPod and he raised his eyebrows in mild surprise. It looked like the line-dancing instructor was trying to keep up with Julia.

Ricardo threw back his head and laughed. When he opened his eyes again, he stopped immediately. Julia's arms were crossed, her foot was tapping. "This was supposed to be a surprise."

The instructor took the intrusion as an opportunity. He wiped his forehead with a towel, took a swig from his water bottle and walked outside for a break.

"What's so funny?" Julia demanded when Ricardo chuckled again.

"Not funny, darlin', just delightful." He sauntered toward her and she rubbed her arms as if a sudden chill had invaded the room.

The glare disappeared and she licked her lips. "I find you more than delightful, too, Ricardo." She held her hand up and waited.

He slipped his arm around her waist. She rested her hand in his palm and he brought them to his chest. "I like the look of these." Without taking his eyes off hers, he tapped her brown cowboy boots with the toe of his.

"Know a better way to get in the mood?" she asked innocently. She looked up at him, her eyes inviting him to test the boundaries.

"Oh, I can think of a few ways." He pulled her against him so that she would have no doubt he was seriously thinking of great alternatives. He would serenade her on any dance floor. And beyond the dance floor, whether with the full moon, in bright sunlight, feeling an ocean mist or hearing a Texas drawl, it was all good.

He started a sexy hip sway and she matched his every move. After a few minutes of the excruciating torture, Julia stopped moving.

"There's no music, Montalvo," she said breathlessly. Her chest brushed against him in its own tortuous way as she tried to catch her breath.

"There'll always be music, darlin'." He kissed her long and slow and let the music in his head guide them home.

EPILOGUE

On a bright September afternoon, Ricardo sat next to Julia in the white horse-drawn carriage, an arm draped easily around her bare shoulders.

She glanced down the hill at the studio and restaurant. Tons of guests milled about, waiting for them to arrive. Photographs had taken forever, and she was impatient to get to them. She stroked Ricardo's cheek, and in the simple gesture, found the feel to be a calming influence. "I love you, Montalvo."

"Love you too, darlin'." He turned her hand and kissed her palm. "It won't take much to get used to this."

She snuggled into his embrace and glanced at the top of the next hill. Ricardo had bought them a new home to keep them in the same neighborhood as the rest of the family.

At the studio, he grabbed her firmly around the waist as she gathered the long train and veil close to her and set her gently on the ground.

She looked up at the sign hanging from the awning. Pride and joy surged through her. With her name next to her aunt's, they couldn't go wrong.

Chase stepped through the doorway and swung Julia into his arms. He spun her around. "Woman, you look hot. I mean, beautiful." He set her down next to Ricardo, who promptly wrapped his arms around her. Chase tapped Ricardo hard on the chest. "You're lucky you saw the light, dude."

"I'm lucky you dragged me to it. Dude." They shook hands and then hugged heartily. "I'm lucky I have you for a friend, Chase."

Julia wrapped her arms around both their waists. "So am I."

"Your grandpa's waiting. I'll catch up later. I'm the DJ tonight."

An impeccably dressed Francisco intercepted them. "Wonderful ceremony. And good job on the restaurant."

The two men heartily shook hands. "You came through, too," Ricardo said. "Thanks for pulling strings to help us buy that empty lot up the street. It's the perfect parking lot for the valet service."

"The least I could do after you and Julia compromised and made this business better than the original proposal."

Ricardo looked at the studio. "I think we owe most of this success to Julia, though."

Francisco nodded and squeezed Julia's hand. "The landscaping and walkways were a brilliant idea. If you two ever want to try your hand at politics, we can always use good idea people to make things happen."

Ricardo wasn't about to bite that bait. "I kind of like it right where we are." He winked at Julia.

She kissed Francisco on the cheek. "Thanks for everything, Cisco."

Francisco hesitated and for a split second, a doubt crept into his eyes. It disappeared as quickly as it had come. "Anytime, Julia. Take care of her," he told Ricardo and walked away.

"My turn!" Grandpa shouted. He looked happy and dapper in his tux, despite the wheelchair. The children had attached streamers to it and a sign on the back that read: *Granddaughter Just Married.* He held Julia close when she bent to kiss him.

"*Chiquita,* he was sent here for you."

"I know. I've never been happier." She whispered, "No prenup here, Grandpa. He's the one."

Ricardo took her hand in his and kissed Don Carlos on the forehead. "Have you ever seen anyone look more beautiful than Julia, Don Carlos?"

"Just one, son." His eyes misted.

"I bet she was stunning. Thank you for making me open my eyes."

Ricardo pulled Julia toward the center of the crowd.

Lorenza winked at her. "We need to give Ricardo a little advice for the wedding night."

Ricardo turned crimson and wrapped his arms around Julia. "Save me."

Elvira held up her hands. "No, no. I have nothing to do with this."

"You're no fun," Lorenza chided. "We need some new gossip for a new scandal." She scanned the crowd. "Oh, Chase," she called out, making everyone around them laugh.

Elvira turned to Julia. "Are you ready to give him his gift yet?"

Ricardo glanced at each of the three women. "Should I wear some protective gear?"

Julia grabbed him by the hand. "Not necessary. Today."

They turned the corner of the building, the crowd at their heels.

"Close your eyes."

"I trust you won't embarrass me, Julia."

"Not today. You have my word."

When he closed his eyes, she led him to the studio's sign near the front entrance. "You can open now."

His eyes automatically scanned the poster board stuck in the corner of the window. His smile turned radiant.

Julia spun her wedding ring on her finger. "I made the sign for my aunt when I was thirteen. I updated it yesterday so it would be ready when we come home from our honeymoon. It was the next best thing to etching your name in stone, to make you part of the family forever. That sign's not coming down again."

"It's perfect, darlin'. Just perfect." He kissed her.

The poster board listed dance lessons available at the studio, written in a bold curlicue handwriting. Beneath the waltz, squeezed into the only available space at the bottom of the sign, was an additional new offering: Country Two-Step.

Home, honeymoon, him. She glanced around, surrounded by those she loved, facing a man whose love and promises made her head spin. She reached out and touched his arm, afraid he'd disappear.

Western music filtered through the air.

"That's our cue." Ricardo held her hand and led her through the studio doors. Taking her in his arms, he guided her into a slow two-step rhythm. The crowd formed a circle around them, then couples paired up and joined in.

"Two-step or salsa—the music doesn't matter, darlin'," Ricardo whispered in her ear. "What matters is having you right here." He squeezed Julia close, and his warmth seeped into her.

They were where they were meant to be. She could hardly wait to teach more classes, hire a new instructor or two and keep her family legacy alive. Could she follow in her aunt's footsteps? Julia looked into Ricardo's eyes. Their legacy was just beginning and the thought of it made her heart fill with a happiness she'd never known.

When his lips touched hers, her doubts dwindled to nothing, the crowd disappeared, and her body swayed to the sweetest music she had ever heard.

AUTHOR'S NOTE

Dear Readers~

A favorite quote I keep coming back to year after year is this:

"...in a time lacking in truth and certainty and filled with anguish and despair, no woman should be shamefaced in attempting to give back to the world, through her work, a portion of its lost heart."

~ Louise Bogan

I love my work as a writer. I do the best I can to produce works I'm proud of that readers can relate to. I can't assume I give back to the world a portion of its lost heart, but I can guarantee I put my heart into what I write. ***Salsa Serenade,*** first published in 2000 as ***Serenade***, is the first of a few novels I received the rights back to from Kensington Publishing (*Pinnacle Encanto* imprint) that I will revamp, update and edit because I love the characters. I hope you will too.

There's an undeniable heat between **Julia and Ricardo**, but at the core they show a deeper connection—loyalty and fierce protectiveness of their families. Once their passion comes alive on—and off—the dance floor, sparks really fly and the hard and fast rules of business begin to blur.

Thank you for giving *Salsa Serenade* a read. If you enjoy the story, please leave a review on www.amazon.com

You can also get a glimpse of my other work and the writer's life on:

Facebook:
www.facebook.com/sylviamendozasd
and on my
Website: www.sylvia-mendoza.com

Love & Light,

Sylvia

ABOUT THE AUTHOR

Growing up a Navy brat, Sylvia Mendoza lived in different versions of paradise like Hawaii, Guam, San Diego and—later in life—Puerto Rico. Through all those travels and more, she found peace at beaches and her passions took root. Her most constant source of entertainment was reading, writing in diaries, learning about different cultures, and the fine art of people watching.

The combo led her to write professionally, earning bachelor's and master's degrees in journalism along the way. Firmly believing that every person has a story to tell, writing profiles and features stories—people stories—became her passion.

It wasn't enough. The creative muse—and writing groups—helped her find a delightful outlet writing fiction, non-fiction, poetry, and lyrics.

Now an award-winning journalist and author, Sylvia knows that writing articles inspires her, writing non-fiction educates her and writing women's fiction frees her. When she has to get away from her computer and get the blood flowing again, running near beaches is her favorite stress release. Spin classes, salsa dancing, live music, and dreams of more traveling can also do the trick.

Please visit Sylvia at www.facebook.com/sylviamendozasd or www.sylvia-mendoza.com